"My God," he said. "You're so beautiful..."

As Shauna hastily pulled her kimono closed, she thought that Rob, too, was beautiful. And she'd made a promise, she told herself, not only to Rob but to herself. Now it was time to follow through.

She saw the question in his eyes, and she raised a hand to trace the outline of his jaw. Then she pulled his face toward hers....

But after a moment he drew back. "Shauna," he said, "this is torture. Being here—having you in my arms—you don't know what it does to me."

"I know what it does to me," she said with painful honesty. And she knew that neither of them would sleep that night if she went back to her own room....

Leigh Michaels likes writing romance fiction spiced with humor and a dash of suspense and adventure. She holds a degree in journalism and teaches creative writing in Iowa. She and her husband, a photographer, have two children but include in their family a dog pound mutt who thinks he's human and a Siamese "aristo-cat," both of whom have appeared in her books. When asked if her husband and children have also been characterized, the author pleads the Fifth Amendment.

Books by Leigh Michaels

HARLEQUIN ROMANCE
2657—ON SEPTEMBER HILL
2734—WEDNESDAY'S CHILD
2748—COME NEXT SUMMER
2806—CAPTURE A SHADOW
2830—O'HARA'S LEGACY
2879—SELL ME A DREAM
2951—STRICTLY BUSINESS

HARLEQUIN PRESENTS
 702—KISS YESTERDAY GOODBYE
 811—DEADLINE FOR LOVE
 835—DREAMS TO KEEP
 876—TOUCH NOT MY HEART
 900—LEAVING HOME
1004—THE GRAND HOTEL
1028—BRITTANY'S CASTLE
1049—CARLISLE PRIDE
1068—REBEL WITH A CAUSE
1107—CLOSE COLLABORATION
1147—A NEW DESIRE

Don't miss any of our special offers. Write to us at the following address for information on our newest releases.

Harlequin Reader Service
901 Fuhrmann Blvd., P.O. Box 1397, Buffalo, NY 14240
Canadian address: P.O. Box 603,
Fort Erie, Ont. L2A 5X3

Just a Normal Marriage

Leigh Michaels

Harlequin Books

TORONTO • NEW YORK • LONDON
AMSTERDAM • PARIS • SYDNEY • HAMBURG
STOCKHOLM • ATHENS • TOKYO • MILAN

Original hardcover edition published in 1988
by Mills & Boon Limited

ISBN 0-373-02987-X

Harlequin Romance first edition June 1989

For Pete Reiter
With love and thanks
for being on call at all hours.
The expertise is his,
the errors mine.

CHAPTER ONE

IT WAS probably nothing, Shauna told herself. Children, and especially twelve-year-old girls, often had stomach-aches, and Mandy *had* eaten an awful lot of pizza. It was really no surprise that, by the time she'd been put to bed in the cream and blue guest-room of Shauna's high-rise flat, she was uncomfortable. She had asked for it, that was for sure—ordering pizza with anchovies, red peppers, and onion, and then topping it off with a double-chocolate milkshake!

Nevertheless, Shauna was a little uneasy. Mandy was her responsibility until their mother came home the next day. I should have told the child to order something a little more sensible, she thought. And if Mandy really is sick—what am I going to do about that? And how will I explain it to Mother?

She won't be very happy if she comes home tomorrow to a sick daughter, Shauna reflected, and that was stating it mildly. Nobody actually liked to deal with illness, but it certainly wasn't Jessica Peters's strong point. Jessica had never been the kind who sat at a bedside and bathed a fevered brow. She was more apt to turn the whole problem over to one of the maids and go out to lunch...

Being entirely responsible for an almost adolescent girl for a week was an eye-opener, Shauna decided with a yawn as she got ready for bed herself. And yet, she had really enjoyed spending this time with her little sister. It had taken days to break down the wall of Mandy's re-serve and begin to find out what the girl thought, but once she had started acting like a child, there hadn't been a dull moment. Shauna felt a tinge of regret that the week was over, and tomorrow Mandy had to go home.

She turned out the lights in her bedroom, pulled the curtains back, and looked out on the never-dark city that bustled twenty storeys below her bedroom window. Against the dark current of the Mississippi River gleamed the brilliant lights of the riverboat restaurants that were permanently moored at the foot of the huge stainless-steel Gateway Arch. It was scarcely eleven o'clock, and down there on the riverfront gaiety spilled from the boats in waves, just as the dark river water beat gently against the levees.

'You're becoming an old fuddy-duddy,' Shauna accused herself. Under other circumstances, she might be down there tonight, dancing and enjoying herself, with Greg——

'Don't even think about Greg,' she told herself sternly. But it was a futile order; it was hard not to think of Greg, when—if things had been just a little different—next Saturday would have been their wedding day...

Mandy, she reminded herself. Think of Mandy instead.

She wrapped herself in a silk kimono and tiptoed into the guest-room. Mandy was sleeping restlessly, the blankets twisted as if she had been fighting a battle. But at least she was asleep, and that was the best treatment for the stomach-ache, Shauna thought. With any luck, tomorrow it would all be gone.

In the morning, Mandy was quieter than usual. Her eyes were vaguely shadowed behind the dark rims of her glasses; the strong lenses made her look just a little like an owl. She was eating her breakfast cereal with a notable lack of enthusiasm, and the book beside her place mat lay untouched.

Shauna dropped a casual kiss on the girl's dark hair and pulled out the chair at the head of the table. 'It looks to me as if you're doing more stirring than eating,' she commented.

The housekeeper pushed open the swing door from the kitchen just in time to hear the comment. 'You can say that again, Miss McCoy,' she muttered as she poured Shauna's coffee. 'The little bird hasn't eaten more than a couple of bites.'

Mandy sent a disgusted look up at the woman, and then stared down at her bowl again.

'Is your stomach still hurting?' Shauna asked.

Mandy shook her head without looking up.

'Then would you rather have something else to eat?' Shauna asked gently. 'I'm sure Louise would be happy to fix you an egg, or some fruit——'

Mandy shook her head. 'Oatmeal's fine. I'm just not hungry.'

'After all that pizza last night, I should think not.' The reply was light, but Shauna's eyes reflected concern. She spooned up a section of grapefruit and said, 'I'll drop you off at school before I go to the office, and George will pick you up this afternoon and take you out to the house. He'll stop here and get your suitcase first. Mother should be there by the time you get home.'

Mandy didn't seem to hear. It was as if all her aloofness had come back overnight.

Really, Shauna thought. The child could be more difficult than any two adults. She looked at her little sister with puzzlement, and tried to remember if she herself had been so perverse at twelve. Probably I was, she decided. 'I've really enjoyed having you stay here with me this week,' she went on. 'I'm glad Mother decided to give all the servants a vacation while she and Rudy went to Mexico, aren't you?'

Mandy nodded jerkily.

'I'll call her this afternoon and tell her what a good time we've had.'

Mandy's eyes lifted from the cereal bowl. 'Why bother?' she said coldly.

It was like a slap in the face. 'What on earth do you mean by that, Amanda Abrams?' Shauna's tone was sharp, and she made an effort to soften it. 'I honestly have had a good time, Mandy; I wouldn't lie to you about a thing like that——'

Mandy's face seemed to crumple, and a tear splashed into her bowl. 'I didn't mean that I thought you lied, Shauna,' she said with a quiver in her voice. 'I meant that you shouldn't bother to tell Mother about it. She doesn't care what I do, as long as I stay out of her way.'

'Darling, Mother loves you very much. She just has an odd way of showing it sometimes.' She looked at the child and wondered how on earth to explain it. Now that she stopped to think about it, she remembered all too well what it had been like to be twelve years old and Jessica's daughter—half-child, half-woman, needing her mother the most at the very time that Jessica had pulled away. Shauna had almost forgotten, but now it seemed that the pattern was repeating itself with Mandy. Perhaps, Shauna thought, having this coltish, unpredictable youngster around frightened Jessica.

'I think sometimes Mother hates to be reminded that she's old enough to have a child your age, Mandy,' she said, with a twinge of humour.

Mandy pulled a twisted handkerchief from the pocket of her dark blue school uniform and blew her nose defiantly. 'I don't know why that should bother her,' she said sullenly. 'She has a child *your* age.'

Shauna smiled. 'I think she has completely wiped from her memory the fact that I'm her daughter,' she murmured.

'Until it's handy for her to remember it,' Mandy said, 'so she can dump me off on you while she goes to Mexico with Rudy.'

'Darling, in the first place, you weren't dumped; I invited you. And in the second place, I've loved having you. I'd like to have you stay all the time——'

'Really?' Mandy's face lit up. 'Can I, Shauna?'

Now what do I say, Shauna thought. When will I learn to think before I speak? 'I said I'd like it,' she said carefully, 'not that we could make it work.' She watched Mandy's face fall, and felt like a criminal. 'Mandy, dear, you may feel sometimes that Mother doesn't care about you. Every girl your age feels that way now and then. I did, I know. But it doesn't mean that she doesn't love you——'

Mandy was staring straight at her. 'And besides all that,' she said, very precisely, 'you've got Greg. And as soon as you marry him, you won't have time for me any more.'

Shauna felt as if she had been struck across an open wound. She bit her lip, and then said as calmly as she could, 'Mandy, you know perfectly well I'm not going to marry Greg.'

'Mother says you'll change your mind.' Mandy gave her a sideways look, as if she was gauging her sister's reaction. 'She says you still love him, and you're just being incredibly stubborn. What did he do, anyway?'

'Mother is——' Shauna swallowed the rest of the sentence. There was no point in going on; the fact that Jessica didn't comprehend Shauna's reasons for breaking her engagement was certainly none of Mandy's business. 'What he did is something I do not care to discuss with you, Mandy. At the moment, I am not planning to marry anyone at all, but whether I change my mind or not, there will always be room in my home for you.'

'I know you say that,' Mandy said. It was lifeless. 'But you'll probably be too busy. Can we go now? I don't want to be late for school.' She pushed her chair back, picked up her book-bag, and went to stand by the front door of the flat.

Sometimes, Shauna thought, I would really like to murder this child. She's precocious, she's too intelligent for her own good, and she's just not grown up enough to deal with all the emotional garbage that every child must face these days—especially a child who lost her father when she was so young. The combination makes her very difficult sometimes——

And also very vulnerable, Shauna knew. She suspected that Mandy's prickly attitude was mostly assumed to protect her tender heart, and it made Shauna want to hug her close. This child was a lot like she had been at the same age—more so, sometimes, than she wanted to remember.

She said goodbye at the gate of the private academy that Mandy attended, and when Mandy started to get out of the black Jaguar without answering, Shauna's hand closed on her little sister's shoulder. 'Remember your manners, young lady,' she reminded succinctly.

Mandy sighed, and then said, mechanically, 'Thank you for letting me stay with you this week, Shauna.'

'That's not what I meant, and you know it. Parroting a thank-you doesn't mean anything to either of us. Is that all this week has meant to you? I thought you had as much fun as I did, but I guess I was mistaken.'

Mandy sniffed once, defiantly. Then she flung herself across the car into Shauna's arms. Her convulsive hug loosened every pin in Shauna's upswept auburn hair, and nearly choked the breath out of her.

'We'll do it again soon,' Shauna promised.

'Next weekend?'

'We'll have to check with Mother. She may have other plans for you.' Shauna knew it must sound like a feeble excuse to Mandy, but it would be worse to promise something that she couldn't carry through.

'OK,' Mandy said reluctantly.

The last view Shauna had of her was a small, rigid spine, clad in the same dark blue as the rest of the girls, marching towards the imposing door of the academy. She sighed and put the Jaguar into gear. The only thing that was going to benefit Mandy was time, she thought as she drove back towards town and the new glass and steel building where the accounting firm of McCoy and Associates rented office space. Mandy needed time to grow up, to let her emotions catch up with her intellect and her talent. It would help, Shauna knew from experience, if there was someone who cared enough to listen to her...

I've been too preoccupied with my own concerns to really notice Mandy, she thought. She's grown from a little girl almost into a young lady while my back was turned. I've been so busy managing her trust fund that I'd completely forgotten she's a person with feelings——

I'll have her come to stay again next weekend, she decided as she crossed the luxurious waiting-room of her office suite and closed her own mahogany door behind her. I'm sure Mother won't mind. And it's not just for Mandy's sake, either. It was pleasant to have her with me, because she helped me to laugh again. She filled the hours, and made me forget for a little while that things aren't going to be the way I planned them.

So Mother thinks I'll change my mind and marry Greg after all, she thought idly. Well, Mother is wrong.

Jessica had told her, when Shauna returned her diamond engagement ring, that she was crazy to give up a man like Greg simply because of a single incident in his past. And the worst of it, Shauna admitted painfully, was that at least once every day she found herself wondering if her mother was right. Sometimes the pain of being without him was almost too much to bear, and she questioned whether she should have ignored the past, after all, and married him despite it. Sometimes she rose in the middle of a sleepless night and looked at the wedding gown still hanging in the back of her wardrobe and asked herself if she had done the right thing. 'Any man is bound to have a few indiscretions floating about,'

Jessica had told her. 'Greg's only human, and you're being quite unrealistic, Shauna.'

Was she being too harsh on him? she asked herself. Was she expecting too much of marriage? Jessica said she was, but then, Shauna reminded herself, Jessica had been married five times.

'Her standards,' Shauna told herself drily, 'are apparently a little different from mine.'

She straightened her shoulders and looked out across the city, past the gleaming new buildings that had thrust St Louis's skyline heavenward. Rigid she might be, she told herself, but there could be no compromise when it came to her feelings about Greg, and what he had done. And if her mother was right in saying that every man she met would have a similar skeleton in his cupboard, then Shauna would do without men altogether. There were worse things in life than being alone.

In any case, she knew she could never again be hurt the way Greg had hurt her, for she would never again give her trust so easily into the keeping of another human being. It was some relief, she told herself, to know that she would never have to feel this kind of pain again.

She was still standing at her office window, looking east towards the Mississippi and trying to concentrate on the relative merits of investing in treasury bonds or precious metals, when the intercom on her desk buzzed.

'I'm sorry to disturb you, Miss McCoy,' her secretary said, 'but the nurse at Mandy's school would like to talk to you.'

Anxiety gripped Shauna's throat. Had the stomach-ache turned out to be appendicitis? Or had Mandy been injured somehow? She had only been at school for an hour—what could have happened in so short a time?

Half an hour later she was face to face with Mandy in the nurse's office. 'We couldn't reach Mrs Peters,' the nurse said. 'There was no answer at all at the house.'

'She won't be back till later today.'

'I am sorry to bother you, Miss McCoy, but I don't think this should wait. It's not the first time that Mandy has come in with stomach pain, you see——'

'Yes,' Shauna said grimly. 'I think it should be checked out, too.' It was obvious to anyone with eyes that Mandy was suffering.

'It doesn't hurt so very bad,' Mandy said, as soon as they were in the car.

'Are you suggesting that I just take you home? Why don't you want to see the doctor, Mandy?'

'It's not that,' Mandy said defensively. 'I like Dr Stevens a lot.'

'But you told me this morning that your stomach-ache was gone, when it obviously wasn't,' Shauna pointed out. 'There must be some reason why you didn't tell the truth.'

It was a very small voice that said, 'Because I hate it when I'm sick. Mother's always mad at me when I'm sick.'

'Mad at you? Why on earth would she be angry with you for something you can't help?' Mandy didn't answer. Because it interferes with Jessica's own plans, Shauna concluded. Or at least, it seems that way to Mandy. 'Well, then, we should be glad that she isn't home yet.' As an attempt at humour, it fell flat, and they were both moodily silent the rest of the way to the clinic.

Dr Stevens was apparently very busy, because the wait—since they had no appointment—was a long one. Shauna flipped idly through a magazine as she watched patients come and go. They ranged from tiny babies to teenagers. It was a large group practice, with half a dozen pediatricians' names listed on the door, and the waiting-room seemed to be always full.

She put the magazine down. She couldn't have told the name of it if she had been asked, anyway. 'I thought you always saw Dr Collins, Mandy.'

'That was a long time ago. I like Dr Stevens better.'

Shauna glanced at her watch. Mandy was apparently not the only one who preferred him, she thought drily, judging by the length of the wait.

A nurse took them back to an examining-room. 'Why do you like him so well?' Shauna asked idly. It wasn't that she cared; she was only trying to keep the child's mind off the delay.

Mandy shrugged. 'I don't know.'

'There must be something special about him.'

'He doesn't have cold hands,' she said finally.

Shauna supposed that made sense. To a child, medical degrees wouldn't have much meaning; things like cold hands would.

The door opened and a young man in a short-sleeved striped shirt came in. One of the patients' parents has barged into the wrong room, Shauna decided. It must be just a baby, though, she concluded, because this was an athletically built young man who couldn't have been much over thirty. His sun-streaked blond hair looked as if he'd just come in from a windy street.

Mandy held out her arms. The young man gave her a hug. 'What's up today, Mandy?' She put a hand silently on her abdomen, and he said, 'Yes, they told me you're having another stomach-ache. What are we going to do about it?' He turned to Shauna. 'I'm Rob Stevens. And you are——?'

'Shauna McCoy—I'm Mandy's sister.' Mandy was right, she reflected; his handshake not only wasn't cold, it was warm and strong and firm.

'Her half-sister, right?'

'Yes, if you want to get technical.' She said it coolly; what difference did it make to him, anyway!

'It's the hair,' he confided. 'You certainly don't look much like sisters.' Before she could gather her wits, he was talking to Mandy again.

Shauna occupied herself with memorising the pattern of the wallpaper, only half listening to the murmured

conversation. When he spoke to her again, she was surprised that he even remembered she was there.

'When did this pain start, Miss McCoy?'

'Last night. She ate an awful lot of pizza, but——'

'I doubt it was the pizza. Mandy, I'm going to have
to take some blood——' It was gentle, but the tone of
voice brooked no argument. Mandy scowled.

A nurse put her head in the door. 'Doctor, there is a
telephone call for you. I wouldn't bother you,
but——'

'Who is it, Jane?'

The nurse looked at Shauna as if she was unwilling
to say anything in front of her, and then sighed. 'It's
the electric company about your bill. It's overdue again.'

'You tell them that if they shut off the power in my
apartment one more time, I'll sue them,' he said, but it
was calm, as if it didn't bother him much. 'I mailed them
the money.'

'Are you certain?' Shauna asked idly.

'I beg your pardon?' Dr Stevens asked.

'I just wondered. You have a blue envelope in your
hip pocket, you see, and it looks awfully like a utility
bill.'

His hand went to his pocket. The expression on his
face as he stared down at the unstamped envelope was
the funniest mixture of surprise and chagrin that Shauna
had ever seen. He gave it to the nurse, as if he was
washing his hands of the problem. 'I'll need you to help
with this exam in a minute, Jane,' he said.

She looked at the crumpled envelope and sighed. 'I
just hope I can explain this in a minute,' she said in a
long-suffering tone, and let the door drop shut behind
her.

Rob Stevens sighed. He looked a little embarrassed.
'Bills,' he said. 'It isn't the money I mind, it's the paperwork. And I would have sworn I'd paid that in time.'

Shauna stopped being quite so amused. What kind of a doctor was he, she wondered, if he couldn't remember details like electricity bills?

'Would you mind stepping out into the hall, Miss McCoy?'

'Why?' she asked baldly.

'Because I'd like to talk to Mandy alone for a little while.'

'That's ridiculous. Mandy, you don't care whether I'm here, do you?' She took a step towards the examining table, and somehow, even though he hadn't seemed to move, Rob Stevens was in the way.

'It is not up to Mandy to choose whether you stay,' he said. 'My primary concern is my patient, and I think it would be better for Mandy if she can talk to me privately.'

My eye, Shauna thought. He just wants me out of here, no matter what excuse he has to use. She picked up her Gucci bag. 'I am very sorry that I embarrassed you by finding your electricity bill,' she said sweetly. 'I promise not to tell anyone about it.'

He didn't answer; he held the door for her instead. The nurse was coming down the hall. 'Jane, would you show Miss McCoy to my office, please?'

Shauna sat in the cramped little office for what seemed hours, tapping the toe of her Italian shoe on the carpet. What in heaven's name could they be doing to Mandy? she wondered. It was taking for ever.

Finally she couldn't bear to sit still any more, so she paced the floor and examined the room. According to the framed diploma that was the only thing hanging on the wall, his medical degree was from a prestigious university—probably a fluke! Shauna decided. The desk was covered with papers, magazines, and folders, though she had to admit they were in neat piles. On the floor behind his desk, in the corner, was a stack of frames. 'That figures,' she muttered. 'He's probably forgotten all about them, too. I wonder how many years he's been here, and when he'll get around to hanging his pictures up.' She wondered how his family felt about being relegated to the floor. Perhaps they'd grown used to it, she decided. Who knows, she thought; they might even like living by candlelight!

He came in just then and shut the door.

'Don't doctors wear white coats any more?' Shauna asked irritably.

'Not in this office.' He pulled his desk chair around and sat down. 'It frightens the little kids.'

'I'd say you'd frighten more of them with that tie.'

He looked down. 'What's wrong with this tie?'

'If you don't know, I couldn't possibly explain it to you.'

'Miss McCoy, there is no need to be sarcastic. I asked you to leave; I didn't throw you out of that examining room.'

'Oh? Then why do I feel bruised?' Her tone was flippant.

He looked at her for a long moment, his blue eyes like ice against his tanned face. 'You deserve to, you know,' he said grimly. 'How dare you put that child in that position?'

The sudden attack stunned her. 'What position?'

'You didn't leave her any choice in the matter. What was she supposed to say—"No, I don't want you, get out"? If she hadn't asked you to stay, you would have been furious with her.'

'Well, you certainly took care of that.'

'Yes, I did.'

'Now, are you going to tell me what's wrong with her, or is that between the two of you, too?' She knew she sounded nasty, and she didn't care.

'I'll tell you. Some adult needs to do something—I suppose I'll try you first. I'm ordering a few more tests, but as best I can tell, there is nothing physically wrong with Mandy.'

"It's all in her head?'

'Not exactly. In any case, I hope you'll remember, Miss McCoy, that psychosomatic illness is no less painful simply because it doesn't have a physical cause.'

'I have a college degree, Doctor. Of course I know that.'

'Letters after a name don't have anything to do with common sense, Miss McCoy.'

She smiled and struck back. 'You should know,' she said sweetly. 'But then we all have our own definitions of common sense. Mine includes paying my bills on time.'

He ignored the jab, and she felt a little ashamed. 'Mandy's pain has been going on for several weeks,' he said. 'In a case of this type, the first thing we suspect is trouble at school.'

'Mandy? She's an honours student.'

'I know. I talked with the headmistress at the academy a few minutes ago, and she says there is no problem at all. That leaves Mandy's other activities, and her home life. She's been staying with you for the last week, I understand?'

'Yes,' Shauna said crisply. 'And if you're implying that I've been beating her or something——'

He shook his head. 'Please, Miss McCoy. I don't suspect anything of the sort.'

That was some consolation, she found, and she was a little ashamed of herself for jumping to the conclusion that she was being accused.

'If you had been mistreating her,' he went on smoothly, 'she'd have had symptoms earlier in the week.'

'Why, you——'

He went on ruthlessly. 'On the whole, I'm inclined to think that she's miserable at home, and that's what's causing her pain. She doesn't want to go back there.'

'Did Mandy tell you that?'

'Not exactly. Mrs Peters seems to be a very cold woman——'

'Are you suggesting that Mother is abusing her?'

He shook his head, but his eyes were watchful. 'There is no evidence of physical abuse.'

'Well, if you're talking about neglect, you're off base. Mandy has everything she could want. She's an extraordinarily sensitive child, and like every girl, she sometimes has problems getting along with her mother.'

'You sound as if you know what it's like.' His tone was bland. 'Did you also have trouble getting along with your mother?'

'We aren't discussing me, Dr Stevens. When I need psychoanalysis, I'll go to a specialist.'

'Miss McCoy, I only meant that there is something in Mandy's home environment that is upsetting her badly, and I thought perhaps you could help explain it.'

Shauna shook her head. 'Doesn't Mandy know what's bothering her?'

'If she could face it, talk about it, and deal with it,' the doctor said drily, 'she wouldn't be having stomachaches.'

That's elementary psychology, Shauna, she told herself. She felt a little ashamed of herself for not realising it.

'She said her mother is coming home today.' When Shauna nodded, he said, 'I'd appreciate it if Mrs Peters would call me.'

'I'm sure she will.'

'I'm not.' He reached for a prescription pad. 'I've been Mandy's doctor for nearly a year, and I haven't met her mother yet.'

Shauna blinked in astonishment. 'Then how do you know she's——' She stopped herself short. She hadn't come here to discuss Jessica's character defects; family matters should stay in the family, she reminded herself.

It was a lesson she had learned long ago—more from Jessica's bad example than from her teaching.

He looked as if he'd like to pursue it, and Shauna said quickly, 'Then how does Mandy get here?'

'Sometimes the housekeeper brings her. Or Mrs Peters' maid. I haven't seen the chauffeur and the gardener yet, but I expect to make their acquaintance any day.'

'Oh,' Shauna said softly. 'I didn't know that.' It wasn't exactly a shock, though, she reflected. It sounded like Jessica. Her time would be too valuable to spend waiting for a doctor's appointment.

'I'm not surprised.' His hand skimmed across the tablet's surface.

He was left-handed, she realised, and he wore no ring. Had wedding rings for doctors gone out along with white jackets? she wondered. On the other hand, she couldn't imagine any woman putting up with the electricity being shut off on a regular basis... Restrain your curiosity, she told herself firmly. It's certainly none of your business.

'Here are the orders for a few additional tests I'd like to do, just to be certain.' He tore off the top sheet and handed it across the desk. 'Would it be possible for you to take her over to the hospital right now? It will take a couple of hours, I'm afraid.'

'That's no problem.'

He smiled. It was quite a charming smile, Shauna realised.

'I'll let them know you're coming, then, so there won't be any more delay than necessary.'

'Thank you,' she said, feeling a little awkward. It had been more than an hour, she realised, since he'd first walked into that examining room, and he had shown no impatience, no hurry, even when she'd been sarcastic. There were probably dozens of people waiting for him, too, as she and Mandy had waited. 'I appreciate everything you've done.'

'That's my job.'

'I'm sorry I was a little——' She paused, and then decided it was better not to go into detail. She picked up her handbag. 'By the way, about your electricity bill——'

'Yes?' The single word was clipped. He had risen from his chair.

She was sorry she'd brought it up, but it was too late to back out now without looking like a total fool. 'I'm a certified public accountant,' she said lamely. 'One of the things my firm does is personal financial assistance—we pay people's bills, do their personal record-keeping, that sort of thing. If you're interested——' She held out a business card.

He looked at it. 'Really? Do you do a lot of it?'

At least he hadn't taken offence, she thought with relief. 'Mostly, it's for people who have run up bills too enormous to pay,' she admitted, 'so they give us their pay cheques each week, and we take care of keeping the creditors away from the door while they get back on their feet. But there's no reason we couldn't help you out.'

'And my electricity won't ever be turned off again?' He sounded intrigued by the possibility.

She raised a hand. 'I'll personally guarantee it.'

He laughed, then. It was a nice laugh, she thought, low and infectious. 'Don't make idle promises,' he warned. 'This war's been going on for a year, you know. But I may take you up on that offer.'

CHAPTER TWO

JESSICA'S house, sprawled on a couple of acres in an exclusive suburb just west of St Louis itself, looked like Hollywood's interpretation of a Southern colonial mansion. Shauna visited it as seldom as she could manage, and she always tried not to look at the gleaming white façade, with its huge pillars and imposing portico, as she came up the winding driveway. Something about the proportions of the place offended her, and she always half expected to see a camera crew on the lawn, with a director about to yell, 'Action!' It was more movie set than house, which really shouldn't be a surprise, she reflected, considering that Jessica's current husband, Rudy Peters, had produced last year's most financially successful Hollywood film, and had won an Oscar for his trouble.

The butler ushered them into the front hall. 'Mr and Mrs Peters are having cocktails on the terrace,' he said. 'I'll——'

'Thank you, Willis. We can find our way.' Shauna brushed by him before he could argue about etiquette. Her heels clicked against the polished black and white marble floor of the hall.

Beside her, Mandy giggled, for the first time all day. It sounded a little out of place in the cavernous hallway. 'I love it when you put him in his place, Shauna.'

'I don't do it out of meanness, you know,' Shauna warned. 'It's not Willis's fault that he's a stuffed shirt—Mother demands it.'

'Terrace' was a loosely-used term at the Peters' home; it was more like a screened porch, Shauna had decided

24

long ago. Jessica's delicate complexion was too easily damaged by the sun, she declared; the truth was, Shauna believed, that her recent facelift did not bear up as well as she had hoped under harsh lights. Besides the sun, the very thought of flying insects was enough to send Jessica screaming to her bedroom. So the terrace was actually just another room, with one wall screened with fine mesh to let in the soft spring air, and shades over the mesh to filter the light into gentle pastel patterns.

Jessica was lying on a long chaise. Her lavender peignoir trailed across the purple upholstery and on to the flagstones, looking as if a sculptor had arranged each dainty fold. She lifted a hand, dripping with rings, as Shauna and Mandy came in.

'Darlings,' she murmured pathetically. 'It's so good to see you. No, don't hug me, Mandy. Mummy's very tired from her trip.'

Baby talk, yet, Shauna thought, as if Mandy was three years old instead of twelve!

'Kiss me carefully, pet,' Jessica ordered. 'Don't muss my hair—I just haven't the energy to sit still while my maid fixes it again.'

Shauna's hand was resting on Mandy's shoulder; she could feel the tension building in the child's muscles. There was a mulish expression on Mandy's face that might have been scorn.

'Did you have a good time with Shauna, dear? I'm sure you did. Wouldn't you like to go up to your room now, Mandy?' Jessica asked. Her voice was languorous, a mere exhausted breath, but there was a thread of steel under it that demanded obedience. 'I'm sure Nancy has your supper ready.'

Mandy gave Shauna a long, sad look and a dutiful hug, and went off. She had not said a word.

Shauna took a deep breath. I'd like to shake the woman, she thought. Can't she see what she's doing to that girl? Rob Stevens had been right—Mandy was miserable here, and with good reason. No wonder the child was making herself sick.

And yet, was that being quite fair to Jessica? Perhaps she *was* simply exhausted tonight. And how could Rob Stevens be so certain that Jessica was to blame? He'd said himself that he had never met the woman. What made him the expert?

You're going around in circles, Shauna, she told herself. Skip the judgements and just give Mother the facts.

Rudy Peters turned from the bar at the far corner of the terrace and said, 'Hello, Shauna. Have a cocktail with us?' He didn't wait for an answer before he put a tall, cold glass into her hand. 'My own recipe,' he said. 'I call it a Rocky Mountain High.'

She tasted it warily. It was good—a mixture of tart and sweet—and she would bet that it was only slightly less dangerous than a glass of hydrochloric acid. 'How was Acapulco, Rudy?'

He grinned and waggled a long black cigar at her. Rudy Peters had made his money in manufacturing top-secret things for the government, and now that he was retired he was dabbling in motion pictures, indulging a romantic streak that no one had ever suspected him of possessing. He was a rotund little man with bushy eyebrows but no hair at all on the top of his head. His expensive polo clothes looked as if he'd slept in them. He was not Jessica's style at all, Shauna reflected, and yet this marriage had lasted longer than any of her mother's other experiments in matrimony.

I wonder why, she thought. He seems devoted to her, and yet sometimes it seems that she barely tolerates him——

'Acapulco was fine,' Rudy said. 'The rest of Mexico was terrific. Jess stayed in the hotel, and I went roaming.'

Jessica shuddered. 'Out in the desert,' she murmured, 'with all the tarantulas.'

Rudy shook his head. 'No tarantulas, Jess. Just a scorpion here and there. I found this great little village that would make a wonderful location for a picture I'm going to finance.' He handed Jessica a glass. 'If you'd like a piece of the action, Shauna, I'm sure I can arrange for you to get in——'

Jessica took a long swallow and said firmly, 'Rudy, darling, could you two talk business some other time? You know how much it bores me to listen to financial details. Shauna, thank you for taking Amanda off my hands this week.'

'I was happy to. Mother——'

Jessica went on, her soft voice relentless. 'It solved all my problems. Now the staff's vacation is all out of the way, too. I hate having different people around me—when they go away one at a time it upsets me for weeks. I have such a delicate constitution, you know.'

'I know,' Shauna said drily. Delicate, she thought. Jessica had buried two husbands and divorced two more. 'Mother, I took Mandy to the doctor today.'

Jessica sighed. 'What now?'

You must exercise tact, Shauna reminded herself. Without it, you are going to get nowhere. 'Dr Stevens ordered some tests. He doesn't think it's anything really serious, but she seems to be troubled about something——'

'Troubled! What does a child her age have to be worried about?'

'That's what he isn't sure of.' Shauna certainly wasn't going to be the one to tell Jessica that Rob Stevens's suspicions had rested squarely on Mandy's mother! 'He'd like you to call him. I'm sure he'll have the test results tomorrow.'

Jessica sniffed. 'He probably wants to send her to a psychiatrist who will sort out all her childhood woes at an incredible charge per hour——'

'He didn't suggest anything of the sort.'

'He will,' Jessica said cynically, 'as soon as he's got all the money he thinks he can get. They give doctors part of the profits from all those tests they run, you know.'

That blithe accusation made Shauna furious. 'Rob Stevens seems to be an ethical, careful, and excellent paediatrician, Mother——' She swallowed the rest of the protest. It wouldn't do any good to tell Jessica that she was quite sure he wasn't fascinated by money, or else he'd take care of his bills on time to avoid the late-payment penalties!

Jessica's eyebrows went up. 'I see you're already on a first-name basis,' she said sweetly.

Which is certainly more than you are, Shauna thought rebelliously; you've never even bothered to meet the man. But she said smoothly, 'If you don't have confidence in him, Mother, why don't you find another doctor?'

Jessica waved a languid hand. 'They're all alike. At least Mandy seems to like this one. You don't suppose that's why she's ill? Because she's got some sort of crush on him?'

'I don't think so. In any case, if Mandy's doctor thinks she needs care, she should have it. It's her trustee who will pay the bills, anyway——'

Jessica sniffed. 'I might have known you'd throw that up at me. Why Sol named you as a trustee for Mandy, when you were scarcely old enough to have control of the money your own father left you——'

'I was as surprised as you were when his will was read,' Shauna said steadily. She had been just eighteen when Mandy's father had died, and Sol Abrams's faith in her ability to help manage his small daughter's financial affairs had touched her heart.

'But to leave me completely out of it,' Jessica complained, 'and put everything in a trust fund, was simply ridiculous, to say nothing of insulting. I am her mother, after all. I should have had a voice in it. To turn it over to you and Richard Cohn, when neither of you were even related to him——'

The key word, Shauna thought, was trust, and apparently Sol Abrams's confidence in his wife had been on the decline when he wrote that final will. But she swallowed the disloyal thought and said calmly, 'I didn't ask for the position. Nevertheless, I am one of Mandy's trustees, and I'm very concerned about her.'

'And don't think the child doesn't know how to use that to her advantage. She's an expert at manipulating people, and I've no doubt she's been working on you all week.'

Poor Mandy, Shauna thought. 'She didn't pull anything over on me, if that's what you mean. And I'd like her to come and stay again next weekend.'

'I don't need to have her spoiled any more than she already is,' Jessica said flatly. 'It's going to be hard enough to get her back into line after this week of indulgence.'

'I haven't indulged her, Mother. She was very sweet all week, and I loved having her there——'

'That's fortunate for you—but I'm sure it was simply the novelty, Shauna. You'd quickly get tired of it. She is the most temperamental child I have ever known,' Jessica mused. 'I should have known better than to marry a concert pianist, and I should have had my head examined before I ever agreed to have his child. It should have been apparent from the outset what a trial she would be.'

I'm glad Mandy didn't hear that, Shauna thought. It would have been a harsh blow to the child's already fragile self-esteem. She felt guilty even listening to it herself. And what about Rudy? Didn't Jessica mind if he heard all this garbage?

Apparently not, Shauna told herself. But then Jessica had never seemed to mind who knew the most intimate details of her private matters. Or perhaps Rudy had learned long ago not to listen at all; if a man married a woman who had four previous husbands, he'd have to turn a deaf ear to the past sometimes, she thought. Rudy was staring out of the window at the landscaped lawn as if he hadn't heard a word. Perhaps it was easier for him that way.

Jessica was still dissecting the past. 'And then Sol went and died on me——'

'Surely you don't think he did it on purpose, Mother,' Shauna said mildly.

'And left me to raise her alone. Sometimes, Shauna, it's more than a woman should have to cope with. If you had ever tried raising a child by yourself, you'd understand how very difficult it can be.'

'It's not easy on the child, either, to lose a parent,' Shauna pointed out softly. 'I know, from experience.'

'That was different.' Jessica's voice was petulant. 'You seldom saw your father after our divorce, and you were a teenager when he died. Mandy was so little that she scarcely remembers Sol. I can't imagine that you think there's a parallel, and if she's been giving you a sob story about missing him——'

'She hasn't.'

'Well, I wouldn't have been surprised if she had. That child has such incredible fantasies, and when she gets a notion into her mind, it's impossible to shake it loose. She's a lot like you that way, Shauna. You were such a sombre child—always seeing things in black and white, with not a bit of flexibility about you, just like your father. And you haven't got over that yet. This whole thing with Greg, for instance——'

Here it comes, Shauna thought with resignation. She finished her drink and set the glass aside. Rudy looked around instantly, an enquiry in his eyes. Shauna shook her head. Apparently, she thought, he isn't as oblivious as I thought. He's hearing every word of this. I wonder what he's thinking...

'Greg is a wonderful young man, Shauna,' Jessica said, 'and you're a fool to give him up. If I was a little younger, I might be tempted myself—he's got such style, and such wonderful manners.'

'And he also has a past,' Shauna murmured, 'that makes his character look less than attractive.'

'Shauna, where in today's world are you going to find a man who doesn't have a past? Any man is bound to have a few indiscretions floating about——'

'An indiscretion is one thing,' Shauna said slowly. 'Being dishonest about it is another. And not telling your fiancée that you have a year-old illegitimate son is unforgivable.'

Jessica sighed. 'Would you have wanted him to compound the mistake by marrying the girl?'

'You never met her, Mother. I did.'

'But now that you know about it, it's no different than if he was divorced.'

It is very different, Shauna thought. But she didn't expect to be able to explain the distinction to her mother, so she remained silent.

'Be careful that you don't keep him dangling too long, Shauna. There are lots of girls after him, and he may not wait around till you've soothed your wounded pride.'

Rudy grinned. 'Oh, I think he'll wait, Jessie. Don't forget that those other girls don't have all the advantages our Shauna does.'

Meaning what, Shauna thought—my money? It was just another fleck of salt on the still-raw wound. Of course Greg had been after her money; she had simply been too blind, and too naïve, to see it then. Greg had a good job and some money of his own, and Shauna had accepted that as ample evidence that he loved her for herself. It hadn't occurred to her till much later that to some people no amount of money was enough. Yes, it had been the McCoy money that had tipped the scales, and made Greg decide to court her instead of any of the other girls who thought he was charming, and handsome, and wonderful.

In the stillness of the nights, she still flogged herself with the knowledge that she had been a fool. But, she reminded herself, she didn't have to sit still and listen to her mother say it. She rose. 'I think it's past time for me to go home.'

'You've made her angry, Rudy,' Jessica said. 'The worst part of being a redhead is the fact that your face shows everything, isn't it, Shauna? It's such a pity that your hair stayed that unfortunate colour. But at least you inherited my eyes—poor Mandy wasn't even that lucky. Must you go? Come and visit us again, dear.'

I can't get out of here fast enough, Shauna thought. And believe me, it will be a long time before I come back.

But she paused in the front hallway, remembering that Mandy was not as lucky. Mandy had nowhere to go. Shauna was alone in the hall, with not even a servant around, and she slipped up the stairs as quietly as she could and tapped on the door of Mandy's room.

Certainly no one who saw Mandy's surroundings would have any cause to believe that she was mistreated. The big bedroom looked out over the rolling lawn behind the house, and the long windows opened on to a private terrace. The room had been decorated by an expert, in a cheerful blend of autumnal shades that suited Mandy's dark colouring.

Mandy was lying on her stomach across her bed, clutching a ragged teddy bear. Her eyes were closed, and there were wet streaks on her face and tearstains on her glasses. Her dark hair lay in rumpled waves against her thin cheeks. She turned her head away when Shauna came in, but she didn't open her eyes.

Across the room a stereo system, the best brand made in the world, was playing a record. Shauna listened for a moment and sighed. There was no mistaking that par-

ticularly sensual touch on the piano keys as the concerto
rang out through the room. Of all the musicians in the
world, only Sol Abrams had been able to make a piano
sound quite like that. In a way, she thought, Mandy was
lucky. Not many fathers left such a solid memorial, such
a keepsake and reminder for their children.

If only, she thought, Mandy can see it that way some
day.

She sat down on the edge of the bed and put a gentle
hand on the girl's shoulder. Mandy buried her face in
Shauna's lap.

'I want to come home with you,' Mandy choked.

'I know, darling. I know.' She sat there for a long
time, stroking Mandy's hair, and wondering what on
earth she could do about it.

Her own apartment, after a week of Mandy's company,
felt empty, and she was haunted by the memory of the
girl's sad eyes. Her housekeeper watched as Shauna
wandered from room to room and finally said, 'You're
lonely for the little miss, aren't you?'

Shauna nodded. 'Louise, I'd like to bring her here to
live.'

'What does Mrs Peters have to say about that?' Louise
was wielding a feather duster over the bronze statue of
a shepherdess that occupied a corner of the living-room.

Shauna fluffed up a cushion in a corner of an antique
loveseat. She didn't answer the question; instead she
asked, 'What do you think of the idea, Louise?'

'Since you asked, I think you'd be a lot better off to
leave Miss Mandy right where she is——'

'You don't understand, Louise.'

'And get married and have a couple of kids of your
own. Raising children alone is no picnic. I did it with
three of them, and I know.'

Shauna looked at her in exasperation. It must, she thought, be the first time in years that Louise and Jessica had agreed on anything!

Her piece said, Louise took her duster back towards the master bedroom. Shauna sat down in a wing-backed chair in the living-room, stared out into the crisp blue sky where a jet was descending slowly on its final path to the airport, and turned it over in her mind.

Would her mother ever agree to let her take Mandy? It didn't seem likely, since Jessica hadn't even considered letting her come back for the weekend. But wasn't it possible that her refusal was simply misplaced maternal devotion? Jessica might not be the best mother in the world, or the one Mandy would have chosen, but Shauna had no doubt that she loved the child in her own way. It might be a careless and selfish sort of love, instead of the storybook variety, and Jessica might demand that her servants take care of Mandy, instead of doing it herself. But her image of herself as a mother would not, Shauna felt, allow her to hand the child over completely. As far as Jessica was concerned, Mandy's environment was just fine. And there was Rudy; he certainly wasn't Sol, but he was kind enough to the child, in an abstracted way.

Shauna nibbled on a manicured nail and tried to decide why it was bothering her so much. Mandy was certainly not the only child to grow up in a home that was less than ideal. She was not being physically deprived, and she was getting the best education available in St Louis at the academy. Many a child would consider herself in heaven if she could step into Mandy's shoes. With Shauna's support, and that of the excellent teachers at the academy, there was no reason for Mandy's emotional growth to be stunted, even if Jessica was a distant and remote parent.

And yet, Shauna thought, I'm scared for her. She's not like me. I turned to the maids and to my grandmother, and I was fine. Mandy just holds it all inside.

I wish, she thought, that I had married Greg. Then Mother might have agreed to let me take Mandy...

For an instant, it actually didn't register. Then, when she realised what she had been thinking, she began to feel slightly queasy. Did she, down deep, really want to change her mind about him, and back down from that rigid rejection? Was she actually considering using Mandy as an excuse so she could have Greg and her pride too? she asked herself desperately.

She finally had to tell herself to stop acting like a child. She hadn't married Greg, and she wasn't going to, no matter what. She couldn't. Not after what he had done...

She closed her eyes in a futile effort to fight off the pain that washed over her. The pleasantly quiet living-room had faded, and she was back in the lobby of her office building on that dreadful day two months ago when the young woman had come up to her with a child in her arms, just as Shauna was leaving work. The woman had asked if she was Miss McCoy, and then said, 'I thought someone should tell you, before you marry Greg, that this is his son. I think you have a right to know——'

She hadn't wanted to believe it. Not Greg, she thought. Not this.

But there had been no arguing with the documents the young woman presented. And Greg hadn't denied it. He had merely said that he didn't understand why such a little thing was so important to her...

No, she could never feel respect or love for Greg again. No matter what happened to Mandy, marrying Greg was certainly not an alternative.

And some day, she told herself, with more hope than conviction, it will stop hurting so much.

* * *

She was in her office early on Friday morning, doing her usual thorough reading of the *Wall Street Journal*, when her secretary buzzed.

'I'm not ready for my first client, yet, Susan,' Shauna told her.

'I know. But there's a young man out here——' The secretary sounded a bit bemused. 'I'm not sure what to do with him. He doesn't have an appointment, but he said something about you offering to take care of his bills.'

Shauna smiled to herself. So Rob Stevens had come after all; it had been four days since she had made that offer, and she had almost given up on him. Not that it had been keeping her awake nights, that was sure; still, she hated to see anyone in financial trouble, and she suspected Rob Stevens might be. 'Tall, blond and blue-eyed, and his hair looks like he just came in out of a windstorm?'

'That's him.'

Shauna folded the newspaper neatly and pushed it aside. 'Send him in. And bring in a pot of coffee, please. I have a feeling I'm going to need it.'

He was carrying a battered briefcase, and his tie was every bit as loud as the one he'd been wearing the day she first saw him. She wanted to pull it off and throw it into the wastebasket. Instead, she rose and offered her hand.

'Your secretary has already told me I should have got an appointment,' he began.

She stifled a smile. 'That's all right. The electricity company called again, I presume, and you remembered that you hadn't done anything about the bills.'

'No, it was the car repair place.' He sounded harried. 'My car was in twice last month, and I forgot to send a cheque. I suppose the sensible thing would be to trade the stupid thing in on a newer one, but——'

'But you haven't had time to look,' Shauna murmured.

'It's not that. I've had that car since I was a teenager, and I feel disloyal about junking it now.' He looked harassed. 'It's stupid, I admit, but if you knew the things it's got me through——'

'You amaze me, Dr Stevens.'

He snapped open the briefcase locks and dumped the contents on her desk blotter. 'I just picked up everything I could find lying around my apartment,' he confessed.

She looked at her desk with horror, and said, as calmly as she could, 'You mean that you actually haven't been evicted yet?' She turned over a couple of unopened envelopes, noted the postmark dates, and winced. 'I don't suppose you brought your cheque book.'

'Right here.'

She flipped through the register and said, 'Didn't you ever learn to balance this thing?'

'Of course. I just can't remember when I took the time to actually work through it all.' He shrugged. 'And every month when the bank statement comes, it just gets more complicated, so I tell myself I'll catch up on my next weekend off...'

'And somehow that time never comes. I see. Well, let's start with the basic information—your income, your debts, your regular monthly bills...'

An hour later she sat back in her chair, rolled a pencil slowly between the tips of her fingers, and looked at him steadily over it. Then she said, 'Have you any idea what a tangled condition your finances are in, Dr Stevens?'

'Somewhat,' he said. 'It sounds pretty bad, doesn't it?'

'Not impossible, but bad, yes. You've been in practice for almost a year——'

'Technically, I've only been an employee of the practice,' he corrected.

'Yes, I understand that young doctors often start that way. But now you've been offered a chance to buy a share of the practice and be a full partner. That's a big step.'

'I know. A very big step, costing very big money. Which I haven't got.'

'It's the only sensible thing to do, you know. As a salaried employee, you'll never get anywhere. Once you have a full share of the practice, you can soon get on your feet.'

He didn't sound convinced. 'Where is the money supposed to come from?'

'Borrow it. You just have to have confidence in yourself, Dr Stevens. If you don't, who will?'

'But I'm already up to my ears in debt. Medical school was an expensive hobby.'

Shauna looked down at the worksheet on her blotter, where Rob Stevens's finances were laid out in cold black and white. Expensive—yes, he could say that again. How on earth did someone run up forty-seven thousand dollars in debt getting through college and medical school? she wondered idly. Weren't there scholarships for people like that? And it was going to cost him another forty thousand-odd to buy into the practice... Well, that wasn't her problem. She could understand his hesitation, but becoming a partner, no matter what it cost, was still the only sensible thing for him to do.

'If it bothers you so much,' she asked, 'why didn't you choose some other field? Selling real estate, perhaps, or driving a truck——'

'I want to work with kids.'

'So? You still didn't have to go to medical school. You could have started a day-care centre——'

He scowled at her.

Shauna said mildly, 'I'm not trying to be silly. I'd really like to know.'

'Because——' He hesitated, and then the words came out in a rush. 'Because I'd like to think that I can make a difference in the world. I can't create world peace, or solve the problem of hunger. But I just might save the life of a kid who will grow up and do those things. I'm a damn good doctor, Miss McCoy——' He stopped abruptly, as if he'd said a whole lot more than he had intended, and shifted uncomfortably in his chair.

'Then there's not a reason in the world why you shouldn't take a gamble on yourself, is there?' Shauna said calmly. 'I realise that you're concerned about this debt, and of course you'll be years clearing it all up.'

'Years?' he said ruefully. 'I'd sort of hoped to have it out of the way sooner than that.'

'We'll set up a reasonable payment plan. But you can't simply ignore other things in the meantime. You need an investment programme right away, for instance.'

'Investments?' He looked at her as if she'd gone completely mad.

'You don't have to be rich to save money, you know, and since you have only yourself to support, you should be able to live very well indeed and still put some away for the future. With the partnership, you'll make more than enough extra money to pay back the loans.'

'You sound a lot more certain than I feel.'

'I am certain. I can prove it to you on paper, if you'd like. The problem is, you've been handling your money badly, and if that continues it won't much matter what you do. Do you want to pay me to take care of your finances for you?'

He looked ruefully at the legal pad that lay in front of her. 'You couldn't possibly do any worse at it than I have.'

'That's quite true,' she said briskly. 'Actually, I'm considered to be something of an expert. If you'd like a reference, ask Mandy. I made six thousand dollars for her trust fund yesterday morning before I saw my first regular client.'

'Mandy should be grateful.'

'I don't think she cares a rap,' Shauna admitted rue-fully. 'And it's just as well—she's a little young to be thinking of money, anyway.'

'How is she?' he asked suddenly.

Shauna sighed. 'I've talked to her every day, and she seems to be all right, but it's hard to tell. She keeps everything inside.'

He nodded gravely. 'That's the problem.'

Shauna waited, but he didn't say any more. She sup-posed he couldn't tell her much, ethically, but she would have liked to know the results of those tests, and whether Jessica had called him yet. It was an awkward silence. Finally she put her pencil down and refilled her coffee-cup from the carafe on the corner of her desk. 'It must feel as if you're putting your entire life into my hands, but I assure you it really isn't as risky as it sounds. There are safeguards, you know, to keep me from embezzling your fortune.' She raised her eyes from the surface of her coffee.

He was, as she had expected, studying her with nar-rowed eyes. 'What fortune?' he said drily. 'The general public thinks that doctors make tons of money, but I'm beginning to suspect that's not quite the case.'

'You're probably right, and besides, we all like to spend just a little more than we make. But with appro-priate tax planning, and some judicious investments, I think you'll be pleasantly surprised.'

'All right,' he said finally. 'If it's good enough for Mandy, it's good enough for me.'

She told herself there was no point in feeling tri-umphant. She hadn't won a victory, after all; she had just taken on a very large job. 'I think you'll be pleased with the results. Another cup of coffee?'

He looked at his watch and shook his head with a grin. 'I'd better get to the clinic,' he said, 'and start seeing patients—or you won't have any funds to play with at all.'

She laughed and watched as he went out, and then turned her attention to the mass of papers on her desk with a sigh.

Why, she asked herself, did I let myself in for this? You're a do-gooder, Shauna McCoy——

Her usual sort of client was more likely to be trying to avoid the penalties he owed the Internal Revenue Service for last year's unpaid taxes. Well, perhaps it would be refreshing to deal with utility companies and car repair places—she turned over another envelope— and florists, instead. It would be a pity if a young man like Rob Stevens ended up bankrupt because his devotion to his job didn't leave any time to exercise common sense where money was concerned.

His financial affairs were a real mess, an affront to her orderly mind. That could be solved, given enough time and patience. In six months, a year at the most, she could have him well on the road to financial stability, assuming that he didn't acquire a luxurious lifestyle or an expensive wife in the meantime. With a budget and a spending plan, he could probably handle everything himself, then. Simply paying his monthly bills really wasn't a sensible use of an accountant's time, and the service was going to cost him a bundle...

She frowned at the stack of bills and pushed them into a folder. Of course, she'd have to teach him how to do it, or he'd be right back to carrying the electricity bill around in his pocket instead of mailing it. But there would be plenty of time to deal with that question, she told herself, once she had the mess straightened out.

She sighed. She had a feeling that his cheque book alone would be enough to give her nightmares...

CHAPTER THREE

MANDY called her at the office that afternoon. In the background, Shauna could dimly hear the bustle of the academy as classes were released for the day.

'Are you going to pick me up?' Mandy began excitedly. 'Or should I take a cab downtown?'

'What do you mean?' Shauna pushed aside the income-tax worksheet she was struggling with.

'George isn't here with the car to pick me up. I thought that must mean Mother changed her mind about letting me stay with you this weekend, and that you'd be along to get me——' Mandy's voice trailed off miserably.

'No, darling. I don't know what happened to George, but Mother hasn't changed her mind. She told me yesterday——' Shauna took a deep breath and decided to make the situation sound as positive as she could. 'I asked her again, and she said that after a whole week apart, the two of you had lots of things to catch up on. And she said something about taking you shopping for some new clothes for summer——'

Mandy groaned.

'You liked shopping with me last week,' Shauna reminded.

'That was different. We went to fun places, and you let me pick out what I wanted to try on.'

Shauna put one hand to her forehead, where a tiny pain was beginning to throb. 'In all fairness, Mandy, I have to remind you that I wouldn't have let you buy most of what you tried——'

'I know that.' Mandy's tone of disgust was far more mature than her years. 'I just wanted to see what I looked like. And when you asked what I thought about something, you listened to what I said. At least,' she added doubtfully, 'I thought you were really listening.'

'Of course I was, Mandy. It was you who would have to wear the clothes.'

'Mother doesn't listen. She asks me, and then she gets mad when I tell her what I think. So most of the time I end up sitting in a chair and reading a book while she decides what I should wear.'

'That sounds pretty boring,' Shauna commiserated.

'It is. I don't know why she bothers to take me along.'

Then Shauna caught herself up short. The truth was, she remembered, that Mandy had beautiful clothes; if there was one area in which Jessica's taste could be depended on, it was fashion, and Mandy's wardrobes bulged with lovely things. Was this what Jessica had meant, about how easy it would be to allow Mandy to manipulate her?

Well, whether Mandy was intentionally twisting the truth, or whether she had simply chosen this as the most convenient way to express anger at her mother, there was no sense in Shauna adding fuel to the fire.

'Mandy,' she said, 'I don't think I should get in the middle of your disagreements with Mother. When I was your age, I couldn't agree with her on what I should wear, either, but now that I've grown up, I realise that she has much better taste than I do.'

'That's because clothes are the only thing she thinks about,' Mandy muttered.

Shauna bit her lip. She'd like to agree with that, but she also knew she shouldn't encourage Mandy. 'I think you'd better get off the telephone and go out to the front gate. George is probably there waiting for you by now.'

'Are you mad at me?'

'Of course not. But I think perhaps you're letting yourself get a little carried away. You may not agree with

Mother about what you should do this weekend, but surely you don't think she's doing this to punish you?'

'Not exactly,' Mandy said. 'But——'

'Make the best of it, Mandy. Be as pleasant as you can, and show Mother that I was a good influence instead of a bad one, and maybe next weekend she'll let you come and stay with me.'

'All right.' But it was a weak, lifeless response, and as Shauna put the telephone down, she wished that she could just give Jessica a good shaking. Mandy needed a hug, and some attention, far more than she needed more clothes, and if Jessica wasn't going to provide it herself, she could at least allow someone else to take care of it...

You're just upset about the whole world this afternoon, she told herself. It's not Mandy that's bothering you—it's that little voice, nagging at the back of your mind, reminding you that if things had only been different, you wouldn't have been in the office at all today. You would have had lunch with your bridesmaids, and gone to Julio for a manicure. Then you'd have gone home and packed the last of your things, and got ready to go to the church for your wedding rehearsal. And tomorrow, you would have married Greg——

She went back to work on the income-tax problem, doggedly determined to get this worksheet done. But today the figures didn't hold their usual magic for her. There was no allure in making the columns balance, in watching the numbers march precisely down the page in even order to the correct conclusion.

The income-tax worksheet was for an estate that a lawyer friend of Shauna's was trying to settle. Normally, Shauna would have sealed the finished report into a big envelope and told her secretary to drop it off at Andrea's office, but she decided to take it over herself instead.

She hadn't seen Andrea in a couple of weeks, and today she needed the comforting presence of a friend.

And that, Andrea Cohn certainly was. Half of St Louis had been aghast when Andrea, twenty-four years old and fresh out of law school, had married Richard Cohn, who had still been a bachelor at the age of fifty-one. The other half had admired her brass at pulling off a feat that more than one young woman had tried without success. Only a few of their close friends—like Shauna, who had introduced them—realised that Andrea adored Richard Cohn. She would have married him, Shauna suspected, even if he had been a convenience-store clerk instead of the most successful attorney in St Louis.

Shauna thought the whole thing was wonderful; Richard was not only one of her favourite people, but he had been Sol Abrams's best friend and he was the other trustee of Mandy's property. Richard himself still looked bemused about the whole thing, Shauna thought, as if he didn't quite understand what had happened to him. His life had been organised into such neat little packages, until Andrea had come along...

Andrea was in the library at the law office, books piled into a wall on the conference table in front of her, her glasses on her nose, the jacket of her white suit tossed over a chair, and a handful of pencils stuck at odd angles through her dark hair.

Shauna paused on the threshold. 'I'm sorry,' she said. 'The receptionist told me to come back here—I had no idea you were swamped.'

Andrea looked up with a smile. 'She's got instructions that I'm never too busy to see you. Besides, I'll be here all weekend anyway. I'm glad you came in to give me a break.' She tossed her pencil down. 'Is that my client's income tax?'

Shauna handed it across the table. Andrea glanced at the bottom line and said, 'Well, it's not as bad as I expected. You must have done some creative accounting in there somewhere.'

'Me? Andrea, you know I always take a conservative view of the tax laws.'

'I appreciate getting it back in a hurry.' Andrea leaned back in her chair. 'Why don't you let me take you to dinner, as a thank-you? Just us girls. We'll go burn up the town.'

It sounded wonderful, and Shauna appreciated the thought. Bless Andrea's tact, she thought, for not bringing up her broken engagement; of course Andrea had not forgotten what this day should have been. 'Wouldn't Richard mind being left out?' I should talk to Richard about Mandy, she thought. He might have some ideas.

'Richard's in New York, negotiating the sale of a company for a friend of ours. He'll be back Monday, if I'm lucky.' She sighed. 'And if he isn't, I'm going to sue the friend for alienation of affection.'

Shauna laughed. 'You'll feel better after a glass of wine and a plate of fettucini.'

'I hope so. You have no idea how lonely it can be when——' Andrea winced. 'Sorry. That was tactless of me.'

'Please, don't treat me as if I'm breakable,' Shauna begged. 'I have to get over it some time.' And please heaven, she added silently, it will be soon...

But it wasn't to be made easier for her. She had just rolled the first strands of fettucini on to her fork when she looked across the room and saw Greg, at a table full of men.

Andrea followed her glance. 'Damn,' she said succinctly.

'I suppose I shouldn't be surprised,' Shauna said. 'We were planning to have our rehearsal dinner here, and Greg had already reserved a private dining-room for his bachelor party afterwards. I suppose he's having it anyway.'

'Pretty tasteless of him.'

Shauna shrugged. 'It's his favourite restaurant too. If he wants to come here with his friends——' Her voice broke, and her fingers tightened on the fork. Deep inside, every cell was quivering. Why did he have to come here tonight? she was screaming inwardly.

'Do you want to leave?' Andrea murmured.

Shauna shook her head. I can't run away, she thought.

She hadn't even seen him since that last bitter quarrel, the day she had told him she knew about the child, and insisted that he take back the fancy diamond engagement ring she had worn with such pride. He had tried to call her several times, but eventually he had given up. Tonight, it looked as if he was celebrating something, without a care in the world...

'Do you ever wonder if you did the right thing?' Andrea asked quietly.

'Not really. What he did, Andrea——'

Andrea looked unhappy. 'I know it was awful, Shauna. But if you really do love him——'

'Not enough to overlook that.' She bit her lip, and then said, 'It's not just the fact that there was a child, and he didn't tell me. But the mother of that baby had to take Greg to court, Andrea. She had to force him to admit his responsibility, and to pay child support, and he's still never seen that little boy. He says he doesn't intend to. That's what I couldn't forgive. A man who could turn his back on a child——'

'I quite agree with you. But I only wondered if you had changed your mind, and didn't know how to back down.'

Shauna shook her head definitely. 'I've had four step-fathers, Andrea. Some of them were wonderful people— I adored Sol Abrams—but some of them...well, I'd just as soon not think about the racing-car driver any more.

Thank heaven Mother saw the light and divorced him.'
She sipped her wine. 'And I hardly saw my own father
at all. I don't want that to happen to my children. I'd
rather not have kids at all than subject them to that sort
of life.'

Andrea nodded understanding.

Shauna looked down at her plate, where fettucini
steamed silently. It was no longer inviting. 'Let's go,
Andrea. I don't think I can eat, after all.'

She crossed the restaurant, leaving Andrea to deal with
the importunate waiter, heartbroken because of their
neglected dinner. She made a conscious effort not to look
towards Greg's table; perhaps, if she was lucky, he would
never know she had been there.

But he caught up with her at the door. 'Celebrating
your freedom?' he asked genially.

'Not exactly.'

There was a momentary silence, and then he said, in
a husky whisper, 'I've been waiting for ever for you to
come to your senses, Shauna.'

'Not for ever.' She kept her voice cool and level.

'Perhaps it only seems for ever when I'm away from
you.'

'It's been two months, Greg. That's hardly a lifetime.'

'Then you've been counting the days, too.' He caught
her hand, and held it tightly against his lips. 'Darling,
I love you so much! It's been agony, knowing that you
couldn't really mean it, when you said those things. But
now——'

'I meant it.' She tried to tug her hand away. He would
not release it.

'But surely, now that you've had a chance to consider
it, you realise that the past means nothing to us. You
needn't worry about it haunting us. The child support
payment is an irritation, I grant you, but we'll never
miss the money. And I would certainly never allow it to

become an embarrassment—it isn't as though I'd want to take the child into our home, after all——'

'I'd feel better about you if you would,' she said clearly. She pulled away from him. 'I don't care to see you again, Greg.'

'But you love me——'

'I'm afraid I don't believe in love any more. At least, not the kind of love that would allow a man to treat an innocent child like that.'

He was still smiling, but his eyes were furious pools. 'You know what is really behind this, don't you, Shauna? My past was only an excuse. You're afraid of marriage. You're a frigid female, just like your mother, and——'

'And if you were to ask my advice right now,' Andrea Cohn said clearly, 'I'd suggest that you shut up before you're sued for slander.' She took Shauna's arm. 'Goodnight, Greg.'

'You never did like him, did you, Andrea?' Shauna asked as they waited for their cars to be brought around to the door.

'No. But that's beside the point. You wanted him, and that was good enough for me. I've never forgotten, Shauna, that you were the only person who didn't think I was crazy—or a fortune-hunter—for wanting to marry Richard.'

'That's different. Richard's a saint.' The valet brought Shauna's Jaguar to a halt under the canopy with a screech.

'Would you like to come home with me?' Andrea asked. 'I'd offer to come with you, but Richard will be calling.'

Shauna shook her head. 'I'll be fine.' In a way, she thought, it would be like a salve to her wounded heart to be alone, not to have to keep up her defences any more.

The flat was dark. Shauna kicked her shoes off and threw herself down on the couch in the little den. She was too angry to cry, and too hurt to reach out for comfort, and absolutely horrified to find that eight weeks without him had not made it any easier to bear. Seeing Greg tonight had been like ripping dried bandages off a crusted wound. She lay there for a long time, dry-eyed and miserable.

Was he right? she asked herself. Was she afraid of the commitments that marriage required?

It was only an excuse to cover up his own bad behaviour, she knew, and yet the accusation had stung like truth. It would be no wonder, she admitted. After watching her mother make a joke of matrimony, it would be no surprise if Shauna herself had trouble working up the nerve to risk it. Jessica's five marriages would be enough to give any sane person pause.

And what if Shauna was like her mother, underneath?

'I'm not,' she denied fiercely. But could she be sure of that? Certainly, no woman wanted to think of herself as shallow and selfish, and completely unsuited to marriage. But how would she really know until she tried? And then it would be too late to change her mind.

Marriage was a wearing experience; it took two people of unusual stamina to make it through all the trivial quarrels and petty disagreements. How was she to know if she had that kind of strength?

'What difference does it make?' she asked herself wearily. 'You know darn well that Greg doesn't have it. Whether you do can't possibly matter right now.'

Eventually, she must have slept, exhausted by the turmoil of the day. When the telephone started to ring, she jolted upright and reached for it, and then deliberately took her hand away. It would be Greg, she was sure; he had had time to get home, pace the floor for a while, and become thoroughly angry—angry enough to want to finish the diatribe that Andrea had interrupted. Since he couldn't get past the doorman in her building without Shauna's permission, the worst he could do was to call her up. And since she had no intention of talking to him ever again, she let the telephone ring. Why, she asked herself, hadn't she had the damned number changed weeks ago?

'As soon as it stops,' she said, as she tried to ignore the shrilling, 'I'll take it off the hook, and that will be the end of Greg.'

But it had to stop ringing before she could do that, and it looked as if it wasn't going to. Twenty rings, twenty-five—she was furious herself by then, and she grabbed it, knocking a stack of books to the floor. 'Would you leave me alone?' she shouted.

There was dead silence for a moment at the other end. 'I'm sorry if I woke you, Miss McCoy,' said a male voice. It was not Greg's.

Shauna let her head drop back against the arm of the couch as if her neck muscles had been cut, and groaned. 'Sorry,' she muttered. 'I thought it was someone else.' And why, she asked herself, was Rob Stevens calling her up at this hour? 'How did you get this number?' she demanded. 'It's unlisted.'

'Mandy gave it to me. I'd like to talk to you.'

She twisted around and looked at the clock. 'It's nearly midnight,' she said, more to herself than to him.

'I've just come from your mother's house.'

She sat up straight. 'What's wrong with Mandy?' It was an anxious question. For the first time she wondered if the chauffeur had ever shown up at the academy. What if he hadn't, and Mandy had started to walk home? Anything could have happened to a child alone——

'She's all right, for the moment. Look, Miss McCoy, I'm breaking all the rules of ethics to do this, but could I stop by and talk to you about her?'

'At this hour?' Then she caught herself, and added, more reasonably, 'Yes, of course. Did Mandy give you the address, too?'

Poor Mandy, she thought. She's crying out for help. But what am I going to do about her?

She called the doorman and told him that Dr Stevens would be stopping by. 'No, I'm not sick, Walter,' she added. 'And don't bother asking to see his identification—if he runs true to form, he's probably lost his driver's licence.'

Then she splashed cold water on her face and debated whether she should offer Rob Stevens a glass of wine. It might give him the wrong idea, she decided, and then looked at herself with scathing honesty in the long mirror on her bathroom wall. No man in his right mind could think she was attempting to be seductive, she decided as she tried to smooth the wrinkles out of her linen skirt. She gave it up as a bad job and was just pulling the cork out of the wine bottle when the doorbell chimed. She stepped into her shoes, winced, decided she didn't care what he thought, and kicked them off again.

He looked tired. About the same way I feel, she decided. 'Would you like a glass of wine?' she asked.

He shook his head. 'Not on an empty stomach, thanks. I'd probably fall asleep on your floor.'

'You haven't had dinner?'

'No time.' He rubbed the back of his hand across his forehead.

'Come to think of it,' Shauna said, remembering her neglected plate of fettucini, 'I haven't eaten since lunch myself. Come on.'

He followed her into the kitchen. 'You cook?' he said.

'Occasionally. Does it shock you?' She draped her jacket over the back of a chair and put on an apron.

'I thought people who owned apartments in this building all had live-in butlers and maids.'

'Sorry to disappoint you. My housekeeper goes home every night.' She studied the contents of the refrigerator. 'Ham and eggs all right?'

'Sounds wonderful, Miss McCoy.'

'My name's Shauna. Even Emily Post would agree that when you have breakfast in a woman's kitchen at midnight, it's permissible to use her first name. Sit down. How's Mandy?'

He settled into a soft leather chair at the breakfast table. 'You realise that I probably shouldn't be telling you all this?'

'I have a very adaptable memory.'

'All the tests we did this week indicate that nothing is physically wrong with her, but she's still having stomachaches. Tonight was a bad one.'

'Do you often make house calls?'

'You know exactly why I went out there tonight.'

'So you finally got to meet my mother.'

'Yes.'

The single word, she thought, held a world of meaning.

'She seems to think Mandy's faking it.'

'Really? Then why did she call you tonight if she's so certain there's nothing wrong?'

'She didn't. The upstairs maid did.'

'Oh.' Shauna turned a slice of ham in the frying pan. 'Well, I don't have much influence with her. I'm afraid I wouldn't be much success at persuading her to take Mandy seriously, if that's what you want me to do.'

'Not exactly,' he said thoughtfully. 'Have you ever considered taking Mandy to live with you, on a permanent basis?'

'Yes. I'm afraid it just wouldn't work.'

He looked at her appraisingly. 'Why not? Would it be too much trouble for you?'

'You needn't be obnoxious. You suggested it yourself.'

He nodded. 'You're an unknown quantity, of course, but Mandy seems to adore you, and I thought you'd surely be better for her than your mother.'

'Gee, thanks.' It was crisp. 'I'm honoured by your respect for me.'

There was a long moment in which the only sound in the kitchen was the sizzle of eggs in the frying pan. Then he said, 'That didn't come out in the most tactful way, but——'

'It most certainly didn't.'

'It was just that Mandy said you might be getting married, and I thought that might have something to do with your reluctance.'

'There's certainly nothing wrong with Mandy's mouth, is there?' Shauna said bitterly.

'Not if she wants to talk. If she doesn't, it's something else altogether.'

Shauna set a plate in front of him and poured two glasses of wine. 'What does that mean?' She picked up her napkin.

'There is something going on, something that Mandy's afraid of. She would not tell me what it was.' He inhaled the aroma of ham and toast and sunny-side-up eggs with appreciation. 'She'd be more likely to talk to you.'

'Keeping family matters in the family? You underestimate yourself.' Shauna buttered a slice of toast. 'I'll talk to her tomorrow. But as far as persuading Mother to do anything she doesn't want to——' She shook her head. 'I'm not having much luck. I couldn't even get her to let Mandy come here for the weekend. As for allowing her to move in permanently——'

He had cut into the still-sizzling slice of ham. 'From what you said yesterday, there appears to be no shortage of money where Mandy is concerned,' he began thoughtfully.

Shauna looked at him for a long moment. 'I don't believe I like the tone of that question, Dr Stevens.'

He didn't apologise. 'Call me Rob. I was just wondering who benefits if something happens to her. Her mother? You?'

Shauna put her fork down, propped her elbows on the edge of the table, and stared across at him. It was an icy, devastating glare, and bigger men than Rob Stevens had been known to wilt under it. He merely cut another bite of ham and stared back.

'Why do you want to know?' Shauna asked coldly. 'Are you wondering if there's something in it for you?'

His jaw tightened, but he said very calmly, 'I'm only concerned about how best to care for my patient.'

There was a battle of wills across the table, and Shauna gave in first. 'Mandy's father was an extremely successful concert pianist,' she said finally. 'Mandy has a trust fund, and she still gets royalties from his records. If she should die before she's an adult, the money goes to the arts, to symphonies and opera companies, that sort of thing. It's split up in quite detailed terms, and I'm afraid I can't quote the percentages, but if you'd like a list you can talk to Richard Cohn; he was Sol's attorney. I'm sure you know the name.' It was sarcastic.

He merely nodded.

'But neither Mother nor I would get a dime, so you can stop suspecting us of trying to poison her.'

'Abrams,' Rob said thoughtfully. 'A pianist—Mandy's father was Sol Abrams?'

'That's the one.'

'I didn't know that. All it says in her records is that her father died when she was four.'

'Plane crash,' Shauna said briefly.

'I remember now. His private jet collided with a mountain range in California.'

She looked up at him with interest. Sol had been famous, but after so many years, few people remembered the details. 'That's right. He was on his way home from a concert.'

'Tough break for a little kid,' Rob murmured.

'Do you always get so wrapped up in your patients?' She refilled their wine glasses.

He looked startled at the idea. Then he smiled. 'I guess you're right. Every now and then there's a child who seems to be lost, and I can't seem to put him or her out of my mind... But you don't want to hear about that.'

'Of course I do,' Shauna said, and was vaguely surprised to realise that she meant it. She pushed her empty plate away and cupped her wine glass in her hand. Funny, she thought. She'd been hungry, after all.

'That's easy enough to account for. There are six of us kids, and Mom and Dad made a practice of taking in foster children as well, for a few weeks or a few years or as long as they needed a home. So I have about twenty-nine siblings.'

'That does explain a lot.' Including, she thought, his choice of profession, and the tremendous debt for his education. She couldn't imagine the expense, much less the confusion, of that kind of household. 'Thirty of you? In one house?'

'Not all at once,' he added hastily. 'But there was always someone around to talk to, or to have a pillow fight with.' He grinned, and even, white teeth flashed. 'It was sort of like living at boarding-school year round.'

'I doubt that,' Shauna said crisply. 'At least not the schools I went to. Pillow fights were against the rules, and we couldn't even talk after lights-out.'

'That sounds like no fun at all.'

'It wasn't much fun—just a solid education.'

'But lonely,' he murmured.

'Yes, a bit, and I was a long way from home. I scarcely saw Mandy when she was little. It's only been in the last few years that I've got to know her as a person, not just a name on a trust fund to manage.' She frowned. She didn't like the idea that he might think she was a lot like Jessica, after all, ignoring the little girl. But facts were facts. If he wanted a reason to think badly of her, he had it.

He had leaned back in his chair, his wine glass in one hand. 'You must have been awfully young yourself when you took on that responsibility.'

'I'm not the only trustee, of course, and my authority extends only to money—not to personal matters.'

'Mandy thinks you're pretty special.'

'She's a neat kid. Sol was a wonderful man, and Mandy has all his sensitivity. She's not a bit like Mother, who's something of a Sherman tank when it comes to tact——' She stopped abruptly.

Rob didn't comment, but there was a gleam in his eyes that might have been appreciation, and agreement. 'How about his talent? Did she inherit that as well? Mandy told me she takes piano lessons.'

Shauna grimaced. 'She endures them. Of course, she compares herself to Sol, and she thinks he'd be ashamed of her performance. She doesn't really understand yet that he spent years practising.' She yawned. 'You don't have any idea what's bothering her?'

Rob shook his head. He pushed his chair back and started to stack the dishes.

'Don't bother with those——'

He carried them to the sink. 'Old training,' he said. 'I waited tables from the time I was big enough to have a job, and I still can't stand seeing dirty dishes lying around.'

He was awfully matter-of-fact about it, Shauna thought.

'I'll get out of your way now,' he said. 'You look exhausted. Thanks for letting me drop in.'

'Don't rush.' She was a little surprised to discover that it wasn't just a polite protest. Then she noticed the kitchen clock, and was startled.

'I'd appreciate it if you'd let me know what you find out,' he said. 'I'll be at the clinic any time after nine o'clock.'

'But it's Saturday,' she protested automatically. 'And it's almost two in the morning now.'

'It's my turn to see weekend patients. If it's quiet, I'll be out of there by noon.'

'Is it usually quiet?'

'Not that I've seen,' he admitted ruefully. 'But it helps if I think positively about it.'

She frowned. It didn't seem fair, somehow. 'I'll call you after I've talked to Mandy.'

'Good.' He turned at the door and looked down at her, and for the briefest of instants, Shauna wondered if he was going to try to kiss her. She hoped not; he was an awfully nice guy, and she didn't want to have to squelch him.

He reached for her hand, and shook it firmly. 'Thank you for the food and everything,' he said, and was gone.

She stood in the doorway for a moment, looking down the hall with a puzzled frown. Then she shook her head to clear it. And to think I was concerned about him acquiring an expensive wife, she thought. With that technique, he'll never get married at all. It didn't occur to her to think that she was contradicting herself.

It would be a shame, she thought. Some child would miss out on a wonderful father, that way.

She slept heavily, when she finally got to bed, and woke to the shrill of the telephone again. She pushed back the satin sheet with a moan and reached for the receiver, wanting to throw something at whoever was waking her at this unconscionable hour.

It was Rob Stevens. Shauna groaned at the sound of his voice. 'What time is it?' she demanded.

He didn't answer. 'I think you'd better come out to my office just as soon as you can.'

She sat up straight. 'Mandy?'

'Mandy,' he agreed grimly. 'This time, she's run away.'

CHAPTER FOUR

'WHAT do you mean, she's run away?' Shauna repeated blankly. This must be a nightmare, she told herself. I can't really be awake. But sunlight was pouring in the window of her bedroom, and the clock on the bedside table was remorselessly ticking away the seconds while she tried to clear her mind. No, it wasn't a nightmare. 'Why would Mother have called you about it, before she even let me know Mandy's missing?'

'Nobody called me. I don't think they've missed her yet.'

Shauna's head was really spinning now. 'Then how do you know——'

'Mandy was waiting on the doorstep when I got to the clinic this morning, complete with suitcase and teddy bear. She's sitting in my office now, and she says she is never going home.'

'She can be a real Missouri mule when she makes up her mind,' Shauna warned.

'Why do you think I'm calling you? The last thing I need is to be blamed for enticing her away from home.'

'I see your point. I'll be right there.'

Mandy was sitting behind Rob's desk when Shauna arrived. She looked her big sister over coolly, appraising her slightly breathless condition and less-than-elegant clothes. 'Your hair is a mess,' she commented, and turned back to the jigsaw puzzle that was spread out on the desk blotter. She put in a piece and picked up another.

Shauna's hand went automatically to the auburn hair caught up in an untidy knot at the back of her neck. Then she decided that Mandy was merely trying to distract her attention from the problem at hand. 'What on earth do you think you're doing, anyway?' she demanded.

Rob came in. 'It took me half an hour to dig it out of her,' he said. 'I think we'll save valuable time if I summarise.'

Mandy shrugged and kept putting pieces in. It was a puzzle intended for a much younger child; Shauna thought she was probably only working it so that she didn't have to look at anyone.

'Rudy Peters has decided not only to finance a motion picture that's to be shot in Mexico, but to direct it himself,' Rob said.

'That will make it a sure-fire failure,' Shauna muttered. 'I'm glad I didn't invest in it.'

'The picture will be in production for the better part of a year, and the leading man has just announced that he is only available if they start right away, because he's got other work lined up for next year. So Mr and Mrs Peters—and Mandy——'

'Not me,' Mandy said stoutly.

'Will be leaving for Mexico next week, and they won't be back for a year or so.'

'That's utterly ridiculous,' Shauna said. 'Mother would never stand for it. Rudy told me a little about the picture—it's going to be filmed in some primitive little village——'

'Rudy's rented her a whatchacallit,' Mandy said. 'A *hacienda*, I think that's it.' She put the last piece in the puzzle, looked at it critically, and began to take it apart again. 'And he promised there wouldn't be any bugs.'

'He'd have to have an exterminator living in the house, to please her. What I'd like to know, Mandy, is why you didn't breathe a word of this to me yesterday?'

Rob said, 'They only broke it to her last night.'

'That's why George was late to pick me up at school,' Mandy said. 'He had to stop and get Mother's new tropical wardrobe at Banana Republic.' She sounded disgusted. 'I tried to call you last night, Shauna, but you were out. I tried Uncle Richard, too, and there wasn't any answer.'

'He's out of town,' Shauna said. 'And Andrea was having dinner with me.'

'And then my stomach started to hurt.'

Shauna's eyes met Rob's. 'I should say that's no wonder. But why didn't you tell Rob about it?'

'Because her mother was right there,' Rob put in.

'And you didn't throw her out?' Shauna murmured. 'I'm amazed at you.'

'She's a tougher customer than you are,' Rob said. He sounded a little defensive.

'I didn't know what to do,' Mandy went on. 'I thought about it all night, and I decided I'm not going to Mexico, no matter what. So this morning I sneaked out of the house real early and I came here, because I knew Dr Stevens would help me.'

Shauna sat down. Her head was spinning.

'The problem is,' Rob said, 'there's really not much I can do. I certainly can't prove she's being neglected— just the idea that her mother is taking her along would be evidence to the contrary.'

Shauna nodded understanding. 'It could actually be a wonderful opportunity for her.'

Mandy's mouth dropped open. 'You mean you're going to let them kidnap me and drag me off to Mexico?' Her voice was shrill.

'It would hardly be kidnapping. She is your mother, Mandy.'

'But I don't want to go!'

'Would it really be so awful, darling?' Shauna groped for a convincing argument, and said, 'You've been studying Spanish. Just think of the practice you could get, and it's only a year——'

Mandy's eyes brimmed with tears. 'I knew you'd say that. I knew you'd tell me to just make the best of it. That's what you told me about this weekend, too!'

'There's a difference,' Shauna said.

'That's right,' Mandy said triumphantly. 'There's a lot of difference! A year is for ever. Besides, Rudy said there was another picture he wants to do after this one, and Mother wants to move to Los Angeles, and I'll never get back to the academy!'

'Mandy, there are some things that you just can't fight. Families move, and sometimes not everyone is happy about it——'

'Shauna,' Rob interrupted quietly, 'I think you're overlooking something. If this was a warm and supportive family, I'd agree that a year in Mexico might be a wonderful opportunity for Mandy. But under the circumstances——'

Shauna paused to imagine it. Mandy's life in an isolated region of an unfamiliar country, with only Jessica for companionship, deprived of the people she depended on for support, would be agonising for the youngster. 'I'd rather go to prison, myself,' she admitted.

'Mother doesn't really want to take me,' Mandy volunteered. 'She just doesn't know what else to do.'

'Surely there is some reasonable alternative,' Rob said.

Shauna sighed. 'Such as living with me, you mean?'

'It's only for a year,' he pointed out gently. 'You said that yourself.'

She wanted to stick her tongue out at him; how dared he use her own words against her like that? 'I'll try,' she said. 'Come on, Mandy. We have to go talk to Mother.'

'I'm not going back there.'

'Mandy, you have to. You have to tell her yourself how you feel, or she's never going to believe that I haven't just made it up. And I can't simply take you home with me without her permission—I have no legal authority. I'm the one who would be kidnapping you.'

Mandy turned appealing eyes towards Rob.

'I think she's right, Mandy,' he said gently.

She sighed heavily. 'All right. We might as well get it over with.'

Shauna reached for the suitcase sitting beside Rob's desk, and swore under her breath at the weight. 'What have you got in this thing, Mandy?'

'Just my records and important stuff.'

'It feels like anvils.'

'I brought along some books I haven't read yet,' Mandy admitted. 'And my camera.'

'I don't suppose you remembered clean underwear.'

'Of course I did! I brought two of everything. What do you think I am, Shauna? A slob?'

But the moment of indignation quickly passed, and it was a pale, quiet, and frightened little girl who waited by Shauna's side in the marble hallway, waiting for Jessica to summon them. The Peters household seemed to be running quite normally for a Saturday morning, Shauna thought. It looked as if Rob had been right—they hadn't missed Mandy at all. The child tucked a cold little hand into Shauna's as they climbed the stairs to Jessica's dressing-room, and Shauna pressed it reassuringly and whispered, 'It will be all right, Mandy. You'll see.' Her reward was a tremulous smile.

It was only a matter of presenting things to Jessica correctly, Shauna was sure, and everything would be settled. It wasn't as if Jessica was unreasonable, after all, and if Mandy was right in thinking that her mother really didn't want to take her to Mexico at all, but just didn't know what else to do, it might be very easy indeed ...

Two hours later, when she came back down the stairs alone, she felt slightly dizzy, as if she was going to be sick at any moment. She walked across the marble floor with the precision of a tin soldier, got into her car, drove two blocks away from the Peters house, and pulled off to the side of the street, folding her arms across the steering wheel and putting her head down on them.

At first, it had looked as if Jessica was going to be quite co-operative. She had looked concerned at the idea of Mandy being so unhappy that she would run away rather than go to Mexico; she had even allowed herself to frown quite severely, despite the damage it could do to her delicate skin. And she had said, sounding a little hurt but quite reasonable, that if Mandy didn't want to go to Mexico, of course she didn't have to.

Mandy had flung herself into Shauna's arms with a gleeful scream and a few happy tears as well.

And then Jessica had added, 'I'll talk to the head-mistress at the academy on Monday about boarding-schools.'

'Boarding-school?' Mandy said. She looked at Jessica as if the woman had just grown two heads.

'But you sent her away to school once,' Shauna had pointed out. 'She hated it, and even the head of the school said she shouldn't be there——'

'She's older now, Shauna. I'm sure there will be no problem about enrolling you immediately, Mandy, and you can be settled by the time we leave.' Jessica had turned back to her dressing mirror and picked up her powder puff. 'There are some lovely schools in New England, I believe——'

Mandy had pleaded and Shauna had argued, but Jessica had remained adament. 'The stable environment of a boarding-school will be good for her,' Jessica announced.

'If you're concerned about stability,' Shauna retorted, 'I'm surprised you didn't think about it before you decided to drag her off to Mexico!'

'I had no idea she would react like this. And she would have had me to depend on.'

'And if she stays in St Louis, she'll have me. What's the difference, Mother? You can't get much more stable a life than I have, and she could still go to the academy——'

'Oh, Shauna, surely you see that the child needs discipline. I had no idea she'd got so far out of hand in the few days I was gone.'

Shauna said, quite pleasantly, 'Are you actually trying to blame me for this?'

'Running away is not acceptable behaviour, and it will take a firm hand to keep her in order.'

'Mother, I'm quite sure Mandy understands that living with me will not be a vacation. And if discipline is required, I'm quite capable——'

'Darling, I'm sure you have all the right intentions. And of course you enjoyed playing house last week. But it's far more difficult than you think to be a full-time parent, especially when you're dealing with a temperamental child like Mandy.'

'Why couldn't I be a good parent?' And what, she wondered irritably, made Jessica think she was such a good example when it came to motherhood?

'A woman alone just cannot do the job, Shauna. A child that age needs a father figure.'

'She's not likely to get that in boarding-school,' Shauna muttered.

Jessica shrugged the comment off. 'Many of them have male teachers. And in her case, it's the discipline that's really important, and I think Amanda's behaviour this morning has shown that she has been getting her own way far too much, and has an inflated sense of her own importance. No, Shauna, I'm afraid you simply wouldn't be able to handle it.'

'I would rather die than go to boarding-school again,' Mandy announced.

Jessica eyed her and said, 'That's exactly the sort of thing I mean. Stop dramatising yourself, Amanda, and go and unpack that suitcase.'

Mandy flounced to the doorway. 'I should have known you'd only make things worse, Shauna!' she accused.

Shauna put her fingertips to her temples. Her head was throbbing like a diesel engine.

'Don't slump down in your chair, Shauna, dear. It's so unattractive.'

Shauna sat up, and instantly wanted to kick herself for obeying the command. She wasn't a little girl to be ordered around any more, and yet it looked as if her mother was going to succeed in doing just that.

I am an adult, dammit, Shauna thought. I'm old enough that I could have kids of my own in pre-school, and yet she insists it takes a man to discipline a child properly! My mother is the ultimate chauvinist...

'Just out of curiosity, Mother,' she said politely, 'would you have felt any differently about it if I had actually married Greg?'

Jessica was silent for a moment, while she painstakingly brushed lipstick on to her cupid's bow mouth. 'I might,' she conceded. 'I think a man in the house makes so much difference. But didn't you say that's out of the question?'

'Yes, I did,' Shauna said crisply.

'Well, then, there is no point in discussing it. If Mandy has her heart set against Mexico, then boarding-school is really the only choice. I think it will be good for her.'

There was nothing left to say. Shauna walked out of the dressing-room feeling as if she'd just collided with a ten-ton truck. Mandy was waiting for her by the top of the stairs.

'I'm sorry I said that,' she whispered, 'about you making it worse. I know you tried. It's not your fault she's such a complete——' Mandy bit off the rest of the sentence and threw herself against Shauna in a convulsive hug. 'I'll go to boarding-school,' she said. 'And I hope it's far away, because I never want to live with her again.'

Shauna swallowed the lump in her throat and tipped Mandy's tear-stained face up to hers. 'No matter what it takes, Mandy,' she said, 'I'll make sure you don't have to go. I swear to you, I'll get you out of this.'

Then she had kissed Mandy's cheek, and smoothed the dark hair, and marched down the stairs and out of her mother's house like a tin soldier...

'All right, Shauna McCoy,' she said aloud. The words seemed to echo against the Jaguar's windscreen. 'Now that you've made your grandstand announcement, just what in the heck are you going to do about it? Sue Mother for legal custody?'

It sounded good, she concluded, but such a case would take months to work its way through the courts, and in the meantime, Mandy would be in boarding-school somewhere. By the time the whole thing was settled, Jessica and Rudy would be home. No, a lawsuit would accomplish precisely nothing.

She started the car again and drove back to the clinic. 'Dr Stevens is with his last patient,' the receptionist told her with a smile. 'You may go back to his office if you like.'

Shauna sank into a chair in the cluttered little room. It was peaceful here, and quiet enough to think. Was there some easier solution? It would have been so simple, she thought, if only all that mess with Greg hadn't come about. Jessica thought Greg was perfect; she would not have hesitated to trust him with Mandy's upbringing.

As if, Shauna thought bitterly, I would have had nothing to say about it! I believe she'd have preferred any man at all to me, even one who deserted his own child. It wasn't just Greg Mother was thinking about, she decided. If there was any man at all in my life, I believe she'd have agreed. It would certainly be less bother for her than arranging a boarding-school on short notice.

Her head was pounding with the enormity of the idea that she was considering. That's ridiculous, Shauna, she thought uneasily. You simply can't do something like that——

The door opened. 'There's a wonderful feeling about sending the last patient out of the door,' Rob said.

Shauna glanced up at the framed diploma on the wall and turned to face him.

He took one look at her and uttered a low whistle. 'No luck, hmmm?'

She shook her head. Then she looked up at him through narrowed eyes, and said, 'Will you marry me?'

For a moment, she thought he was going to turn the same shade of dull green as his tie. Then he said, 'If I was a drinking man, I'd prescribe a shot of brandy for each of us—to cope with your obvious case of shock. How about some iced water instead?'

'To drink or to pour over me?'

'Whichever works.' He handed her a glass and sat down on the corner of his desk while she drank it. 'I think you'd better tell me what happened.'

'Mother absolutely refused——' She looked up with concern in her eyes. 'Aren't you going to answer that telephone?'

He shook his head. 'The lucky guy who comes in on Saturday morning gets the rest of the weekend off. The answering service will take that in a minute. But if it bothers you to listen to it ring——'

'It does.'

'Oh, yes. I'd forgotten about your reaction to ringing telephones,' he said blandly.

Shauna coloured, remembering how she had screamed at him last night.

'Let's get out of here.' He picked up his jacket and ushered her out the back door to his car. 'We could go to lunch somewhere——'

'Not when I look like this,' Shauna said automatically.

'I see you're feeling better. In that case, how about skipping lunch for somewhere quiet, where you can give me the details?' The car swung out on to the busy boulevard. It was a noisy, rusty, and ancient Volkswagen. Shauna decided that it had probably been blue, once.

'You're very thoughtful, you know,' she said.

'Did you propose to me because you need some thoughtfulness around the house? And haven't you forgotten somebody? Mandy told me you were engaged.'

'I used to be. It fell through.' It was toneless. 'Sorry, I think I must have been having a momentary attack of insanity when I asked you to——' She couldn't bring herself to repeat it.

'That's certainly flattering,' Rob murmured. 'I thought perhaps you had concluded I was suicidal and therefore game to take on any challenge.'

Shauna's face flushed with angry colour. 'If you'd been with us this morning, you wouldn't be joking about it.'

'I'm sure I wouldn't,' he said softly. 'Let's go walk through the Japanese gardens. It will be quiet there.'

For the first time she realised that his choice of streets hadn't been aimless; they were just outside the huge, walled grounds of the Missouri Botanical Gardens.

She looked up at him in astonishment. 'How did you know this is one of my favourite places in the world?'

'I didn't. It's just the best spot I know of to think.'

Inside the garden wall, it was possible to forget that the bustling city surrounded them. The azaleas and the dogwoods were in bloom, forming masses of brilliant colour against the peaceful green of ancient trees. Fountains sang a peaceful accompaniment as Shauna told him what had happened.

By the time she had finished, they had reached the Japanese gardens in the far corner of the park-like enclosure. They stood on a high-arched bridge that spanned a corner of the quiet little lake, and watched a couple of lazy ducks floating on the ripples. 'So it's boarding-school,' she said. 'And that was Mother's last word.'

'There are some excellent schools,' Rob reminded.

'I know. But when Mandy was six, Mother sent her away. The school was highly recommended, but Mandy hated it. I visited her there.' She shivered. 'She was thin and pale—all eyes and nerves. It took a year after she left there to get her colour back and learn to smile again, and another year to catch up with her studies. Without privacy, without time to think and dream, she was a mess. I'm afraid that will happen again, Rob. No matter how good the school, the students are regimented. And she's so happy at the academy—she's doing so well——'

His fingers, warm and gentle, kneaded the tense muscles at the base of her neck. It felt so natural to put her head down on his shoulder and let the drowsy warmth of the spring air steal over her. She stole a look up at him through heavy lashes. 'I don't want to see her get lost again,' she murmured.

For a moment, she thought he wasn't going to answer. 'You want to keep her here, and you think if you were only married—— '

Shauna nodded. 'Is it such an incredibly stupid idea after all?'

'And I'm your best candidate?'

It sounded a little strange, even to her. After all, she had met Rob less than a week ago. Why hadn't she turned to someone she knew better? There were men all around her, men she had known for years—men like Greg, she thought with a shiver.

She could not bring herself to do that. Going to any one of those men and explaining the reasons why she must be married—that alone would be hard enough. Rob understood the danger to Mandy—he'd spotted it long before Shauna had—but she had no illusions about the difficulty of making someone else see it that way. Under the circumstances, a man might well think she was crazy to conclude that Mandy needed protection. And she could think of at least one whose overdeveloped ego might make him believe it was him she really wanted, and that she was using Mandy for an excuse. Stumbling into that sort of mess would be unbearable, she thought.

And if the secret leaked out—if Jessica heard of it— then it would all have been in vain. And all those men knew Jessica. She simply couldn't trust Mandy's fate to one of them. She had learned the hard way that she couldn't trust Greg. Those other men were too much like him—thinking only of themselves, of pleasure, of money.

But Rob is different, she thought. He knows what Jessica really is. He truly cares about Mandy. And perhaps we can make some sort of bargain between us, a bargain that will let him be dedicated and idealistic without having to worry so much about money, and that will leave me free—really free, without the fear of the whole thing exploding under me one day.

If it wasn't for Mandy, she thought sadly, I would never consider a marriage of any sort at all. The cost is too high, and the chances of being hurt are too great. I will not allow myself to owe anyone a debt, ever again. But it would be different with Rob. We can both benefit, because I can offer Rob something, too—I can give him a sort of freedom that would otherwise be years away...

Will he understand? He has to, she told herself fiercely. Because there is no other way than marriage.

'Mandy's so fond of you,' she said. 'And Mother certainly couldn't argue about you being unfit to take care of her.'

'What about you, Shauna?' It was a low, level question.

What did she think of him? She had known him such a short time. She respected his professionalism, of course, and his devotion to Mandy. But surely he couldn't expect her to feel fondness, or anything of the sort—just as she didn't expect him to feel anything like that for her. It didn't matter, in any case, she told herself. The only thing that was important was Mandy.

She stepped away from him, just a little way, and drew an abstract pattern with her fingernail on the wood rail of the little bridge. 'I'd make it worth your while,' she said, and was uneasily aware that she hadn't even come close to answering his question. It was an unfair question, she told herself—a foolish question—one that didn't deserve an answer.

He didn't push the matter. He just leaned on the rail and looked down at the water. She wondered what he was thinking.

She gathered all her poise and added, 'It's not as if it would have to be for ever, anyway. A year would do it, I think. Once Mandy is settled somewhere, I don't think Mother will be anxious to get her back. It would be too much effort, and Mother doesn't like to exert herself. That's why I think she'll agree to let me have Mandy. It will be easier for her than arranging for a boarding-school, and if I turn up with a husband, it allows her to change her mind and still save face. Surely between us we can convince her that we're not going to send a little monster back to her when we get tired of the novelty——'

'A year,' he said thoughtfully.

'Or possibly a little longer,' Shauna said, trying her best to be fair. 'Until they're back home and she sees how well we're doing. After that, if something unfortunate were to happen to my marriage—well, Mother could hardly be horrified at that, could she?'

'I shouldn't think so.'

'I know what an inconvenience it would be, Rob, and as far as compensation——'

'Oh, yes. I thought you'd probably get to that some time soon.' His voice was just a little tight, as if the suspense was bothering him.

'I don't like the idea of paying you to marry me, exactly—— ' Shauna began.

'Neither do I,' he said drily. 'It sounds a little too much like being a gigolo for my taste.'

Shauna giggled nervously. 'But neither is it right to expect you to go to all this trouble for nothing. You'll move into my flat, of course, so you'll be saving all your rent——'

'And I won't have an electricity bill any more,' he interrupted. 'Don't forget that advantage.'

She didn't laugh. 'I think it would be fair if I was to pay off the debt you still have for your education. I know it bothers you to have that obligation hanging over your head, and it would give you a fresh start——'

'You know that's a considerable sum, Shauna.'

'My father left me some money. I can afford it.' She looked up at him through the dark fringe of eyelashes, wondering if she would see a gleam of avarice in his face.

There was nothing of the sort. If he was thinking of this unparalleled opportunity to get his hands on the McCoy money, it didn't show. His eyes were sombrely blue as he looked down at her. 'I never questioned for a moment that you could. Still—— '

'Rob, it's self-protection, really,' she admitted. 'I'm sure my attorney will tell me I have to be realistic—if there isn't any arrangement made ahead of time, I'd be leaving myself open to all kinds of nasty things in divorce court when it's over.'

'Quite true,' he said. It sounded as if he'd bitten the words off in chunks.

'At the same time, it has to be a sensible arrangement—I mean, when we get the divorce, it has to appear to have been an ordinary marriage or Mother would really smell a rat——'

'Spare me the logic,' Rob said. 'I'm already impressed by the speed at which you think these things out.'

Shauna frowned. It certainly didn't sound like a compliment, but she decided it wasn't worth arguing about. 'It would be quite consistent for me to pay off your loan,' she said. 'I've never liked the idea of being in debt, so it would be perfectly normal for me to insist that it be cleared up as soon as we were married. Mother would have no reason to suspect otherwise.'

Rob leaned against the railing. The gentle breeze tugged at his hair. He stared down into the quiet lake, at the huge goldfish which had gathered beneath the bridge to beg food, and said, 'Aren't you leaving a loophole? What if I let you pay off my bills, and then I walk out before the year is up?'

'I'd simply have to trust you to fulfil your obligations, wouldn't I?' Shauna said coldly.

'Ah, yes,' he murmured. 'Trust. I wondered if that entered into this arrangement at all.'

'Of course it does.' It made her just a little angry. 'And you'll have to trust me to live up to my end of the bargain, too. Believe me, I'm going to—I've got a lot to lose!'

'So do I, my dear,' he said, very softly. 'So do I.' He turned away and retreated from the bridge to the path that rimmed the little lake.

She caught up with him on the zigzag bridge that overhung the water. 'Just what did that mean?'

He didn't answer. 'It's a tempting offer, I have to admit, and I'd like to take you up on it. But——'

'If you're worried about my expectations,' she said slowly, 'I haven't any. As long as we kept up a public image, it really wouldn't matter what else we did——'

'Oh,' he said, on a note of ironic discovery. 'It's a marriage of convenience! Separate bedrooms and all that?'

'Of course. What do you think I am?'

'I think,' Rob said very clearly, 'that you've given a lot of thought to the legalities here and not much to the human factor.'

She said coolly, 'Let's get things quite clear. I certainly would not expect or want any kind of a sexual relationship.'

'My dear, you don't have to be in bed to have a sexual relationship. We already have one, in case you hadn't noticed—we have had since the moment you mentioned marriage. That sort of conversation tends to change the way two people look at each other, and the instant they become aware of it——'

'I'm not aware of any such thing——' she began furiously.

He brushed a thumb across her lips, and she shivered.

'Yes, you are,' he said. 'And so am I. I've been thinking for the last hour how much I'd like to take you to bed, and that sort of thing doesn't just go away.'

She could feel waves of hot colour rising in her cheeks, but she managed to say, coolly, 'You're an opportunist, Rob Stevens.'

'Perhaps. I'm also a realist. I'm a perfectly normal man with all the usual desires, and you're asking me to turn them off for a year. I don't think you'd appreciate it if I indulged in any hanky-panky on the side——'

'You make it sound as if you're being asked to give up your harem!'

He grinned. 'I don't have a harem, exactly. By the time a medical resident gets through the week, and then puts in forty-eight hours in an emergency room so he has money to eat on, there isn't much time to develop a social life.'

'Well, then, what are you complaining about?'

'It's different now. I've finally got a little time to call my own, and a little security so I'd feel comfortable about making some new entries in my little black book. And you're asking me to move in with you and live as if you're just another sister. I don't think I can handle it.'

'Personally,' Shauna snapped, 'I wouldn't care a bit what you did in your spare time, but since word does spread about things like that, I'd have to have your promise——'

'I don't think the other women would be the problem. But you—you're another thing entirely, Shauna. I suspect that after a couple of weeks of sharing the same roof with you—and not the same bed—I'd be a wreck. I'd never last a year, so I might as well be honest about it now.'

The warmth in his eyes was almost like a stroking hand on her skin. Shauna turned away and said tartly, 'Please don't give me a line about falling in love with me at first sight.'

'I wouldn't dream of telling you anything of the sort. But normal people have sexual desires, Shauna, and that's a trap either of us could be caught in. It wouldn't be a very good image for your mother if she heard you were messing around, either.'

'I wouldn't think of it.'

'That leaves us with a problem. If we can't sleep with anyone else, and we won't sleep with each other, it could be a very frustrating year of celibacy for us both, Shauna, and what would we accomplish?'

There was no answering that. Of course, men looked at things differently; how many times had Jessica told her that?

'Or are you still so much in love with your former fiancé that the thought of any other man makes you nauseous?'

She shook her head, jerkily. 'That's all over.'

'In that case,' Rob said, 'why frustrate ourselves for no good purpose? We're both intelligent adults. We can take care of Mandy, and have a little fun ourselves, too. It's the only sensible way to handle it. Otherwise, I'm afraid it's doomed, and we might as well give the idea up right now. No hard feelings if you want to call it off.'

Mandy. In all this talk, she had almost forgotten Mandy.

He was right, Shauna told herself. What difference did it make, after all, as long as Mandy was safe? If she couldn't have the glorious kind of true love she had once thought she and Greg shared, then why not take the sort of comfort she could have? And if that was the only way she could protect her sister——

'All right.' It was almost a whisper.

'In that case,' Rob said, 'I'd like to kiss my future bride.'

CHAPTER FIVE

'LET me get this straight,' Andrea Cohn said, pushing her raspberry Danish pastry aside and looking at Shauna in disbelief. 'This is not a sick joke? You're actually going to marry a man you've known for less than a week, so you can take Mandy away from your mother because the kid needs a shrink?'

'She doesn't need one yet,' Shauna corrected. 'But she will if this goes on.' She uncurled herself from the couch and reached for the thermal coffee-pot on the tray in front of her.

'And you're paying him to marry you?'

Shauna frowned. 'I'm paying his med. school debts,' she corrected as she refilled Andrea's cup. 'It's a different thing altogether—sort of like funding a scholarship.'

'Not legally. Frankly, Shauna, I think you're the one who needs the shrink.'

'You're my lawyer, Andrea—not my guardian. Just draw up the papers.'

'Can I finish my Danish first?' Andrea asked with deceptive meekness. 'Or are you planning to tie the knot before lunch?'

'I would, if I could.' I would like to have this all over, Shauna thought; the sooner the better. At least then I'd know... Her slim fingers toyed with the heavy gold chain that lay under the collar of her salmon-coloured dress.

'Shauna, think what you're doing! I know Greg hurt you, but to jump into something like this——'

'This hasn't anything to do with Greg.'

'Are you certain of that?' Andrea's voice was low, almost as if she was afraid to utter the words.

As if, Shauna thought, she was half expecting to be ordered out of the flat altogether. Andrea ought to know I'd never do that, she thought with wry humour. I have to get someone to write up this contract; if she doesn't do it, then I'd have to explain it all to another solicitor, and I'd sooner die than go through this again.

'Yes,' Shauna said, with sudden decision. 'I guess it does have something to do with Greg. I had never considered asking him to sign a pre-nuptial contract, and if I'd married him, I'd have been paying for it for the rest of my life. But Greg taught me a valuable lesson—that's why I want everything in writing.'

'That's not what I meant, Shauna McCoy, and you know it.' Andrea looked across the coffee-table with exasperated affection. 'Are you sure you're not on the rebound? It's possible that you're doing this just to get even with Greg, you know. And are you positive this doctor of yours hasn't manipulated you into this with all the fuss about Mandy?'

'You wouldn't think so if you had seen Mandy lately. Or, as far as that goes, if you'd been in the room when I proposed. I thought Rob was going to faint, for a minute, at the idea of marrying me.' For a moment, Shauna saw a glimmer of humour in it. That's one thing about Rob, she told herself; he certainly isn't a yes-man.

'That's what I mean, Shauna. Hasn't it occurred to you that he came around to your point of view awfully promptly, if it was such a nasty shock to him?'

'It may have had something to do with the money,' Shauna said, with mock seriousness.

'I should think so. The money you're offering him may not be a big sum to you——'

'Of course it's a big sum to me. It's worth it.'

'—but it must look like the earth to him.'

'I hope it does. That was the main reason I offered it,' Shauna said crisply.

'But doesn't it bother you? The fact that he's marrying you only because of the money——'

'Well, I'm only marrying him because of Mandy. At least we have things out in the open. If I'm going to be married for my money—and let's be honest, Andrea; any man who comes along is going to give my bank account serious thought—I'd rather be honest about it than to have all the pretence and the lies...' Her voice cracked, and she stopped abruptly and took a big gulp of coffee. It burned her throat and brought tears to her eyes.

Andrea sighed. 'I'm sorry I pushed,' she said, 'but someone has to tell you the truth. Greg's a scoundrel, but not all men are like him. You've got plenty to offer a man besides money, Shauna, and some day, when the right man comes along, you're going to regret doing this.'

'That's possible,' Shauna agreed. 'Nevertheless, Andrea, I'm going to do it.'

'All right. I give up. If you're determined to go ahead, let's at least make it air-tight, so it doesn't come back at you like a boomerang.' She reached for the legal pad at her elbow. 'We'd got as far as the——'

The doorbell rang. 'There's Rob now,' Shauna said, bouncing up off the couch. 'At least you can see that he's not a con man.'

'I've never yet seen a con artist who looked the part,' Andrea protested, but Shauna was already at the door.

Rob stepped across the threshold and handed her a single long-stemmed yellow rose, and when she looked up in surprise to thank him, he kissed her. It was casual and brief, but the caress brought a flood of colour to her cheeks. 'You don't have to impress Andrea,' she managed to say. 'I have no secrets from my solicitor.'

'Oh?' His deep blue eyes seemed to light with mischief. 'In that case, if I don't have to act like a gentleman for her sake, come back here and I'll kiss you properly.'

Shauna refused to meet Andrea's eyes, but she knew that her friend's eyebrows had gone as high as they could. She fled to the kitchen to put the rose in a vase. Her fingers trembled as she arranged the delicate ferns around the still-dewy flower.

Dammit, she thought. Why did you have to go and embarrass yourself in front of Andrea? There was nothing wrong with that kiss! There was certainly nothing about it that should have made your knees go weak——

And there hadn't been anything off-colour about the one yesterday on the zigzag bridge, either, she reminded herself. It had certainly been nothing that would have embarrassed an audience of goldfish-feeders. And yet, she wouldn't have been a bit surprised if she had absent-mindedly walked straight off the edge of the bridge and into the lake as soon as Rob had let her go. That kiss had made her insides turn the consistency of melted cheese. Oh, he was an expert at kisses, that was sure. She wondered, just a little, where he had learned to be so skilful... Hadn't he said a young doctor didn't have time for much of a social life?

By the time her hot cheeks had cooled and she returned to the living-room, Andrea and Rob seemed to be on wonderful terms, analysing the city's current political crisis. It irritated Shauna to see them so friendly, and she set the fresh pot of coffee down with a thump. 'Shall we get on to business?' she said. There was silence. Shauna poured Rob a cup of coffee and said, more mildly, 'We don't dare be late to lunch at Mother's, since I did sort of manipulate the invitation.'

'Of course,' Andrea said, and reached for the legal pad again. 'This shouldn't take more than an hour.'

'An hour?' Rob asked. 'If all we're doing is making sure that I can't sue Shauna for alimony later, it should be quite simple——'

'We're also making sure that Shauna can't sue you,' Andrea pointed out with a smile.

He shrugged. 'I'll take her word for it.'

Shauna said, 'Please stop trying to make me feel like a rat for protecting myself, Rob.'

His jaw tightened. 'Excuse me,' he said. 'Of course, let's cover all the possible angles. I'd hate to find myself liable for your legal bills, for example.'

'That was quite uncalled for,' Shauna said heatedly.

'Stop it, both of you,' Andrea ordered. 'I haven't time to listen to you argue—though I really should let you fight it out. It might end up that you'd both realise what a ridiculous scheme this is, and give it up.' She eyed them hopefully, but when both faces remained stony, she sighed and started writing again.

Rob wandered off to the other end of the big living-room, studied the statue of the shepherdess for a while, gazed at the satiny stainless steel of the Arch from the window, and finally settled down into a corner with the Sunday *Post-Dispatch*. For the next hour, only the rustle of an occasional page turning even reminded Shauna that he was there.

Finally, Andrea said, with relief, 'I think we've got it,' and read back the document's provisions. 'Anything else, Shauna?'

'I can't think of anything.'

'I'll need a copy of your latest financial statement to attach to this, Shauna. And yours, too, Rob.'

Rob didn't even look up from the Lifestyles section as he said, 'I'm quite willing to waive that. Shauna already knows every gory detail of my financial condition, and I don't see that hers matters under the circumstances. I'm agreeing to make no claim on her, after all——'

'But there has to be complete disclosure in order for the agreement to be legal,' Andrea said.

His face darkened. 'And without it, I could go to a judge later and plead that I had no idea what I was signing away? Oh, in that case, let's be certain to preserve the legalities. A man's mere word obviously has no value at all these days.'

'I didn't mean that I wouldn't take your word, personally,' Andrea said levelly.

'It wasn't you I was talking about, Andrea.'

'I know this whole process feels a little dehumanising,' she said, 'but believe me, it's a good idea to get it all worked out ahead of time——'

'Dehumanising?' Rob repeated. 'I've seen hamburger that had more self-esteem than you two have left me.'

'I've got the financial statements,' Shauna said hastily. 'I'll get them over to your office in the morning, Andrea.'

'That's everything, then,' Andrea said.

'Not quite,' Rob said quietly. 'You've left out something major, you know.' They both turned to look at him in puzzlement, and he added, 'Of course, I would be more likely to think of it than either of you would. You've completely neglected to consider what happens if there is a child.'

Andrea looked shocked. 'You're quite correct,' she said. 'I assumed that you had agreed—since this is only a short-term arrangement——'

He smiled, charmingly. 'Just in case,' he confided.

She swallowed hard and said in her best legal voice, 'Of course you're right that it's foolish to assume anything. But——'

'There aren't going to be any children,' Shauna said, at the same moment. She was so furious she could hardly speak. 'Rob Stevens, you can't honestly believe that I would even consider the possibility——'

Rob shrugged. 'Just in case, I'd like a clause in there, Andrea, that says any children of this marriage will be placed in my custody when it's all over with.'

'That is the most ridiculous thing I have ever heard——' Shauna began.

Andrea shook her head. 'I don't think it would stand up in court.'

'Perhaps it wouldn't,' Rob said. 'And perhaps it would.'

'You simply can't decide things like that ahead of time,' Andrea pointed out.

'Really?' Rob said politely. 'Are children less important than alimony, then, in the eyes of the law?'

'That is not what I meant. In any case, Shauna could fight it. You're only asking for trouble if you insist on putting that in, Rob——'

'Shauna,' Rob mused, 'you said it's a useless clause. I presume that means you're using some sort of birth control already?'

Shauna gasped, and then said stiffly, 'Some people seem to have no hesitation about asking personal questions in public!'

'You did tell me that you had no secrets from your solicitor,' he reminded. 'Are you taking the pill?'

'As it happens, yes, but——'

'Then you have no reason not to humour me. Put the clause in, Andrea. Shauna will sign it—won't you?'

Andrea looked at Shauna doubtfully.

It's a matter of principle, Shauna thought. Giving up the right to a child—it's absolutely inhuman of him to suggest it. But then, perhaps Rob's principles are involved as well. I could hardly blame him for wondering if I might be like my mother after all.

Besides, she told herself, this is just the way he's chosen to soothe his bruised ego. It isn't as if we're talking about a real-life possibility, here; it will never become an issue. So if it makes him feel better, why not be agreeable?

She nodded. 'I'll sign it.'

Andrea sighed. 'All right. I'll call you when the papers are typed.'

'Can you get it done by tomorrow?' Shauna asked.

'Are you sure you don't want it yesterday?' Andrea asked drily. 'When is the wedding, anyway? Or should I be honest and tell you that this sounds more like a merger than a marriage?'

'Friday,' Rob said.

'Not till Friday?' Shauna's voice had gone squeaky. 'But I thought——'

'Shauna, it was hard enough last night to tell my mother that I'm marrying a woman she's never met, in a judge's office instead of in church. Do you really want me to tell her that I can't possibly wait till next weekend so she can come to my wedding?'

She swallowed hard. 'No, I guess not. I'd just hoped to get it over with soon, and keep it very quiet——'

'The two of you, a judge, and a pair of witnesses?' Andrea said drily. 'Next you'll be suggesting that you dash over to the courthouse some time when Rob has a break between appointments.'

'Not a bad idea,' Shauna said stiffly. 'This is only a legality, you know.'

'Look, kids, a private wedding ceremony is one thing, and you can even get by with this ungodly haste by saying that you wanted to have Jessica attend before she left the country. But you'd better at least have a reception. Otherwise, the whole affair is going to look extremely fishy.'

'I suppose you're right,' Shauna said. The complications are beginning to get out of hand, she reflected wearily.

Andrea kissed her cheek. 'I'll talk to Richard as soon as he gets home,' she said. 'We'll help out with a party of some sort. Don't worry, darling. You're not in this alone.'

But I am, Shauna thought, with a tinge of desperation. I am very much alone...

*   *   *

'I don't see what your objection is. It's a perfectly nice tie,' Rob said. He turned the tip up so he could look at it more closely. 'And it's almost brand-new.'

'Where did you buy it? Ringling Brothers' last circus?' Shauna reminded herself that tact would get her much farther than sarcasm would, and added, 'It's not bad, exactly—it's just that this one suits you much better.' She stroked the silk tie that lay on the glass counter in front of her, and peeked up at him through long lashes. 'Would you wear it to lunch at Mother's instead? To please me?' She let her voice quaver just a little.

He tapped the end of her nose gently with a fingertip. 'That's cute,' he said. 'But the *femme fatale* act doesn't fit you very well, Shauna. You do much better when you're being straightforward.'

It made her furious. She pushed the tie across the counter to the sales clerk. 'You want straightforward? We'll take this,' she said. 'And if he doesn't walk out of here wearing it, I'll use to strangle him in the car park.'

'Oh, if you had only told me how determined you were, I would have been happy to oblige,' Rob said, on a note of irony. He pulled off his old tie and began to knot the new one.

The young sales clerk seemed to be having trouble keeping a straight face. He rang up the sale, accepted Shauna's cash, and said, 'Will there be anything else, ma'am?'

She picked up Rob's old tie with two fingers and handed it to the clerk. 'Drop this in the garbage,' she said. 'Or give it a ceremonial burning if you'd rather.' She smoothed Rob's collar over the new tie and tucked her hand through his elbow. 'Now, we've got to hurry or we'll be late to lunch.'

Rob looked longingly back at the clerk, who was still holding the tie. 'I see I'm going to have a managing wife,' he said mournfully. 'I'm going to be a henpecked, haunted man——'

She stopped dead in the middle of the shopping mall's main corridor. There were few other people about, since not many of the shops opened on Sundays. It had been hard enough to find this one, but she'd been desperate. 'Rob, do you really think I'm a nag and a scold?'

'Of course you're not,' Rob said promptly. 'I don't think you'll nag me at all, as long as I immediately do whatever it is you want.'

She chewed that one over, and stayed silent all the way from the shopping mall to the Peters' house. Rob was driving her Jaguar, so she had plenty of time to think.

The accusation had cut her to the quick. Such a picture of her character had never occurred to her before. She had prided herself on not being like Jessica, who ruled her house with tyranny, even though it was expressed in soft and cultured tones. But had Shauna merely chosen a different method to get her way?

I was only trying to help him make a good impression, she told herself. Or was it more than that? Had it been a way of showing Rob that she was determined to be the boss—that, though she might marry him to suit her purpose, he really didn't fit into her life, and he shouldn't get any ideas about his place?

He stopped the Jaguar in the circular drive by the front steps and turned to her. 'Don't be nervous about confronting your mother,' he said. 'The worst thing she can do is refuse to co-operate, and then we'll be back at the beginning, with nowhere to go. But at least we won't have to send telegrams to five hundred people to cancel the wedding——'

Shauna's eyes filled with tears.

'Sorry,' Rob said. He slipped an arm around her shoulders. 'I shouldn't tease about something like that.'

She gulped. 'It wasn't—that.'

He scooped a tear up with a gentle fingertip. 'What, then?'

'Do you really think I'm a—a domineering shrew?'

He swallowed a smile. 'You're a bit set in your ways, perhaps,' he said diplomatically. 'It will take some adjusting for both of us.'

She nodded unhappily.

His fingertips slipped gently over the velvety hollow of her cheek to rest warmly against the side of her throat. 'I think you really are a very pretty, very kissable young woman.'

She made a feeble effort to fend him off, one hand pressed against his chest. 'But I've been crying,' she protested faintly. 'You can't want to kiss me when I'm like this.'

'I can't?' His voice was a hypnotic murmur. 'But I assure you, Shauna, I do.' He pulled her hand away from his chest and kissed her wrist, pressing his lips against the pulse point. 'That's a very inviting perfume,' he said huskily. 'Where else do you wear it?' Without waiting for an answer, he set about finding out.

Her breath was coming quickly, in shallow little gasps as his lips travelled an exploratory path along her throat, behind her ear, across her cheekbone. Her head fell back against his shoulder.

It was all the invitation he needed. Gently, he explored the soft mystery of her mouth, probing, plundering, caressing, until Shauna's world had shrunk to a circle with room enough only for the two of them...

When he stopped kissing her, she said, 'What?' and looked up at him with eyes that wouldn't seem to focus right.

'We're late for lunch,' he reminded. 'The butler is waiting for us.'

Shauna sat up straight, so suddenly that she nearly gave herself whiplash. 'Why, you rotten—he's been standing there watching, and you just went on kissing me, like any common rabble——'

'I don't think he was watching, exactly,' Rob said. 'But it is broad daylight, so perhaps he had no choice. And as for being common rabble, I didn't notice you protesting at the time. You wouldn't want your mother to suspect you'd been crying, would you?'

'What's that got to do with anything?'

'Because all the evidence of tears is gone now. Actually, I may have gone a little too far—you look as if you've been making love.'

'I feel as if I've been mauled,' Shauna snapped.

'I'm sorry; I thought I was more talented than that.' He helped her out of the car. At the top of the steps, by the wide front doors, the butler waited with his nose in the air. 'Are you certain *mauled* is the word you want?' Rob murmured. 'I think that you look properly bridal. You certainly don't appear to be worried about facing your mother, which was the main idea.'

'You planned that!' Shauna accused, in a furious whisper. 'You did it on purpose!'

Rob seemed to consider it. 'Well, yes, I did,' he admitted. 'But I assure you that I enjoyed it a great deal. Does that make you feel better?'

Mandy was thrilled by their announcement; she nearly tipped over her chair in her haste to throw herself against Rob for a hug. Shauna breathed a deep sigh of relief at that; it hadn't occurred to her to wonder what Mandy might say, or if it would be wise to warn her of what was coming.

Jessica was every bit as open with her feelings. 'That's quite ridiculous, Shauna,' she said, and seemed to feel that her announcement should be the end of the subject. Instead, she talked determinedly about Rudy's new picture and how much she wished that she had been able to go to Los Angeles with him for the weekend while he made final arrangements for the film, instead of being stuck in St Louis, packing.

Over lunch, Shauna finally gathered her nerve and broke into the monologue. 'Mother, Rob and I would like to have Mandy come and live with us, instead of going off to boarding-school.'

'You don't know what you're asking for,' Jessica said.

'She could stay at the academy that way, and you wouldn't have to worry about getting her ready for boarding-school on top of everything else you've got to do this week.'

Jessica didn't seem to hear. 'She's been growing more impossible by the day, and looking at that tragic face when she doesn't get what she wants is extremely unpleasant. It would be foolish of you to saddle yourselves with the responsibility.'

'I'm sure we can handle it, together. We want to try.'

Jessica looked from Shauna to Rob, and sighed. 'Why you think you want to marry this—person, Shauna, is beyond me. Last week you told me marriage was completely out of the question.'

'Love sometimes has a way of making fools of all of us, Mrs Peters,' Rob said sombrely.

Shauna sent him a grateful smile across the table. He winked back.

Jessica made a graceful gesture of acquiescence. 'Fools—yes. Well, Shauna, I certainly can't account for it. Unless, of course, you're looking for someone who is Greg's opposite in everything that matters.'

Mandy was stirring her serving of cheese soufflé while she listened; it was beginning to look like sour buttermilk. 'And a good thing if she is, too,' she muttered.

'Amanda, you may leave the table,' Jessica announced.

Mandy pushed her chair back with dignity and marched out of the room.

'You see?' Jessica said. 'She's impossible. A good disciplinary boarding-school——'

'She has a right to her opinions,' Rob said.

'What if your prize school doesn't succeed in breaking her spirit?' Shauna asked. 'You'll have a hellion on your hands when you come home.'

'And just when did you become an authority?' Jessica asked crisply.

'Look, Mother, if Mandy hates the school, she's quite capable of getting herself thrown out. You don't want to be running back and forth from Mexico changing her from school to school, do you? It would be trouble all the time. It would be much simpler just to leave her with us.'

'That's very considerate of you, Shauna. You've obviously thought it all out very carefully.'

Shauna refused to respond to the irony in Jessica's voice. 'Yes, I have, Mother.' She looked across the table at Rob in desperation. He had scarcely said a word since they had come into the dining-room.

He smiled at her—not a humourous smile, but one that sent warmth and reassurance flooding over her. Then he pushed his untouched plate aside and folded his arms on the edge of the table. 'Why don't we get rid of the social niceties, Mrs Peters,' he said, 'and get down to business?'

Jessica sniffed. 'I'm sure you'd be much more comfortable that way. Who are your people, anyway?'

He ignored the question. 'I'm going to give you your choice,' he said. 'Shauna and I want to offer Mandy a home. It's a perfectly reasonable thing for us to offer, and for you to accept. None of your society friends will think any less of you for leaving her with us. But if you refuse that offer, and send her off to boarding-school as a punishment—as we all know it is intended to be— then I must warn you that Shauna will go to court, as one of Mandy's trustees, and ask the judge to give her custody.'

'That,' Jessica said icily, 'is an empty threat.'

'I assure you that it isn't. I suspect any good psychiatrist would conclude that Mandy's mental health would be endangered by this completely unnecessary change, and a judge would probably agree.'

Jessica eyed Shauna with dislike. 'I told you he'd bring a shrink into this sooner or later.'

Shauna crossed her fingers under the table and said, 'Richard agrees with us, by the way, Mother. I wouldn't be acting alone.' She made a mental note to talk to Richard the instant he got back into town.

'That would be the messy way to do it, of course,' Rob went on. 'Once the lawsuit is filed, it takes a great deal of time to work its way through the courts. A judge would be likely to order that Mandy be left with us until the case had been heard. Wouldn't it be easier to just reach a compromise between ourselves, today?'

'And you think a court would actually take my daughter away from me?'

'I think that in the long run it's a dead certainty,' Rob said coolly. 'In the meantime, just think of the publicity.'

'And then there's the money for legal fees, of course,' Shauna added quietly. 'Richard would represent our side, of course. Who would you have act for you, Mother?'

There was a long silence. Shauna held her breath. Jessica's dark eyes burned furiously.

'At least the newspapers would have the facts,' Rob mused. 'All of St Louis would be buzzing with the rumours.'

Finally, Jessica gave a harsh little laugh. 'Oh, have it your own way,' she said. 'I'm certainly not going to allow myself to be blackmailed by an adventurer and an idealistic girl for the sake of an ungrateful child. What difference does it make to me whether Mandy goes to boarding-school or stays here? I'm simply too exhausted to argue about it. But I warn you, if you indulge and spoil her——'

Then what? Shauna wanted to say. You'll leave her for us to cope with? I suppose that would be the easiest way... She wanted to sag gratefully in her chair, but she kept her spine rigid. 'There is nothing personal about this, Mother. I'm only interested in what is best for Mandy.'

'You're a fool, Shauna,' Jessica announced. 'I must admit that it will be a great relief not to have boarding-school preparations to make, along with everything else that has to be done this week. No one has time to worry about new uniforms and things for Mandy. We've been packing every minute of the day as it is.'

'In that case,' Rob said, 'the least we can do is to get out of your way so you can work.' Shauna admired him for keeping a straight face while he said it; she thought herself that Jessica's definition of packing probably meant that she lay on a sofa and thought of things for her maid to do. 'We'll take Mandy with us now, if you don't mind.' He pushed his chair back and reached for Shauna's hand.

'I suppose,' Jessica said nastily, 'that you're all going on a family outing to the zoo!'

Rob stopped in the doorway. 'Come to think of it,' he said, 'that's not a bad idea.'

'The zoo?' Shauna said in disbelief as they sped through Forest Park and into the car park across the street from the main gate. 'I thought you were kidding.'

'After talking to Jessica,' Rob said, 'I thought visiting a female hyena would be reassuring. At least she cares about her offspring.'

'Zoos,' Mandy announced flatly, 'are for little kids.' She dawdled along behind them as they walked to the gate.

'In that case,' Rob told her, 'you really have to help me out, Mandy. I like to go to the zoo, and if I can't get in without a little kid along, I'll never be able to go again. Now if you would just pretend to be less than grown up for the afternoon——'

Mandy giggled. 'You're silly,' she told him. 'But I guess I can do you a favour.' She put her hand in his and gave a little skip.

'I should think so,' Shauna said. 'You owe him one, for getting you out of that house in one piece.'

They walked past the concession stand, and Rob sniffed the air. 'Anyone for something to eat?' he asked. 'None of us had lunch.'

'We should have known, Mandy,' Shauna mocked. 'It wasn't the live animals he wanted to see, it was the hot dogs.'

Despite her protest of being too grown up to enjoy the zoo, Mandy wandered off towards the grizzly bears' environmental pen with a hot dog in one hand and a Coke in the other. Rob and Shauna sat down on a bench nearby. The peaceful stillness of the balmy afternoon became mere quiet as they sat there, and then it turned into uneasy silence. Neither of them seemed to have anything to talk about.

'Thank you,' Shauna said finally. 'For convincing Mother, I mean. I couldn't have done it myself.'

'I had hoped not to have to go so far. I don't like making threats.'

'Well, it worked.' She swallowed the last bite of her hamburger and said, thoughtfully, 'You know, Rob, perhaps we don't have to go ahead with this, after all. I mean, she practically said that she won't take Mandy back on a platter——'

'Are you trying to get rid of me?'

He's not about to let me back out of our deal, Shauna thought. Not till he's got his money, at any rate. She told herself it was an unworthy thought. Nevertheless, it was hard to shake the idea.

'Not exactly,' she hedged. 'But the deal was made to allow me to get Mandy, and now that we've accomplished what we set out to do——'

She couldn't see his eyes, behind the dark sunglasses he wore, but his jaw had a firm set to it that she was beginning to recognise. He looked as if he was considering taking her up on her offer. It left Shauna with a hollow sort of feeling. She stared across the wide pathway to where Mandy was leaning against the barricades, watching the prairie dogs play. She was only beginning to realise what a tremendous responsibility she had taken on. It was up to her now to soothe Mandy's hurts, to mould her into a good human being. What if she had to do it all alone?

Rob grinned at her and shook his head. 'And give up a good thing?' he scoffed. 'Besides, I always did like challenges.'

The tightness in Shauna's throat eased a little. It would help more than she had expected, to have Rob around. He was so good with Mandy, and the child liked him so.

'I'm glad,' she said. 'And Mandy won't be a challenge, really, once she feels secure. She only acts up with Mother because——'

'I wasn't talking about Mandy,' he said. He pulled her to her feet. 'Come on, let's go watch the monkeys.'

CHAPTER SIX

WHITE satin, Shauna thought dreamily, yards and yards of it forming a wide, embroidered train to sweep the cathedral aisle. Handmade lace ruffling delicately about slim wrists and framing a fragile throat. A tulle veil falling from a tiara in which diamonds twinkled, concealing the white face of a nervous bride as she went to meet her husband——

The picture she had dreamily conjured up dissolved with a knock on the door, and Shauna glanced once more at the real reflection in Andrea's dressing-table mirror. There was no white satin, no lace, no tulle, no diamonds—just a severely plain silk dress, the colour of heavy cream, tailored to her slender figure, with her grandmother's double strand of pearls nestled under the collar. Only the white face of the nervous bride was anything like what Shauna had expected her wedding to be.

The knock was repeated lightly, and Andrea came in. 'I thought for a minute that you might have decided to climb out of the window and run,' she said. 'Rob's here, and wait till you see what he's got.'

'I'm afraid to ask. Help me get this hat on?'

Andrea pinned the wisp of silk and illusion to the side of Shauna's head and smoothed the last wayward wisps of auburn hair into place. Then she bent over her friend for a gentle hug. 'I want you to know,' she said, 'that I'm growing quite fond of your Rob. Richard likes him, too.'

'Thanks, Andrea.' Shauna's voice was choked and her eyes were misty. Not that it could make any real difference, she thought; she was committed to this marriage, no matter what her friends thought. But she knew that Andrea didn't lie. The strain in her voice hinted that she still wasn't entirely sold on what Shauna was doing, but at least she was not going to make her friend's path harder to walk. The decisions were long since made, and the pre-nuptial agreements had been signed yesterday in Richard Cohn's office. It was obvious that Andrea knew there was nothing a real friend could do now but offer her love and support.

I'm making it sound more like a funeral than a wedding, Shauna thought with wry humour—as if someone very close to me has died.

'He's got style,' Andrea said. 'Take this, for instance——' She touched the ring on Shauna's left hand. 'You'd better switch it to another finger now, or you'll forget and he'll have to fumble with your wedding ring.'

Shauna looked down at the canary-yellow diamond that nestled on her engagement finger, as if she'd never quite seen it before. The delicate oval stone had a rare beauty, and the triangular diamonds that surrounded it, turning the setting into a sparkling star, emphasised, the unusually brilliant colour. It was a silly, foolish, and completely impractical purchase, and she had told Rob that as soon as he had slid it on to her finger. An engagement ring of any kind was unnecessary, she had said firmly; the gold wedding bands they had selected would be quite enough of a display.

Rob had listened patiently, but as if his mind was somewhere else. When she had paused for breath, he kissed her lightly on the mouth and said, 'It's sweet of you to be concerned about my budget, but you needn't bother.'

'Why?' Shauna asked tartly.

'Because I've got all kinds of money now that I don't have to pay rent any more. Besides, all your friends will expect you to have a ring, and you wouldn't want them to think you're such a cheapskate that you wouldn't even let me buy you one.'

It had left her speechless, which she supposed was precisely why he'd said it. She had tried for a couple of days to persuade him to take it back, but it would have been easier to talk to the diamond itself. So she was still wearing the ring, and it looked as if it was on her finger to stay. She had to admit the thing was beautiful, and all her friends had been duly impressed—and it was just as well that she liked it, she told herself, since Rob had probably instructed the jeweller to send the bill to her!

'Most of the guests are here already, I think,' Andrea said. 'Jessica hasn't shown up yet, though. Shall I let Rob come in for a minute? He wants to see you.'

Shauna nodded. What was that old wives' tale about the danger of letting the groom see his bride before she walked down the aisle? What nonsense, Shauna told herself. Besides, in this case, there wasn't even an aisle...

You're getting crazy, she told herself. The sooner this is over, the better.

For an instant, when Rob came in, all Shauna could see was his eyes, darkly serious, with a question in the midnight depths, as he stood beside the closed door. He was frighteningly handsome, she thought, the kind of man who would never lack for feminine attention. He might only be starting to find much time for women, but they would never lack time for him——

If I loved him, she told herself, and wanted to hold him for a lifetime, I'd be worried already.

'Andrea said you should have a corsage,' he said, 'but I thought perhaps you'd rather have something to hold on to.'

'To keep my hands from shaking? Not a bad idea.' Shauna's eyes dropped to the bouquet he was holding. 'Orchids,' she said softly. There were a half dozen of them, huge white flowers with deep yellow throats and ruffled edges so thin and finely veined that they looked like lace. Orchids, the delicate blooms that she loved best of all flowers. No wonder Andrea had been impressed. And to bring them to her himself—most men, she thought, wouldn't even have considered walking around carrying an armful of orchids...

He put the bouquet into her hands. The gold filigree holder that protected the blooms was warm from his fingers; the heat seemed to radiate to her jangled nerves.

Greg had never known that orchids were her favourite, she thought. In the year they had dated, he had sent her roses, violets, camellias, but never once an orchid... How had Rob known?

Lucky guess, she decided. Or Andrea had told him. Don't be an idiot and let yourself get all sentimental. She said the first thing that came into her mind. 'I paid your bill at the florist's shop this week, Rob. It was really out of reason. Who do you send all the flowers to, anyway?'

He only smiled.

'You should ask them to give you a quantity discount.'

'Don't you think that would take all the romance out of it?' he asked mildly.

Then she really felt like a fool. What was wrong with her, anyway? Even a child Mandy's age would know that he wasn't sending all those gorgeous blooms to his mother, for heaven's sake! And furthermore, it didn't matter to Shauna who had got those flowers. She must be starting to sound like a jealous witch, bickering at him when all he had done was to bring her the most beautiful bouquet of her life.

Tears stung her eyelids. 'I'm sorry, Rob,' she whispered unsteadily.

He smiled down at her gravely and said, 'It's only nerves—I know.' But he made no move to touch her, not even the brush of a finger against her cheek. It left her feeling deserted, betrayed once more by her own quick tongue.

She thrust the bouquet back at him. 'Hold this a minute, would you? I forgot something.' She fumbled in her satin clutch purse and handed him an envelope. She buried her nose in the orchids and watched as he warily lifted the flap.

How would he take it? she wondered. She expected that he would be stunned at first, and then grateful. She'd paid off his loans yesterday, as soon as the pre-nuptial agreements had been signed. This was extra—something they hadn't discussed at all.

It was only a small rectangle of paper, pale gold in colour. He took one swift look at it, and then his dark blue eyes turned reproachfully towards her. 'Shauna, I know you think I should be rewarded for helping you out,' he began.

She nodded. 'That's right.'

'But I happen to believe that this is excessive. Not even you can have forty-five thousand dollars lying around in pocket change, for God's sake——'

The delicate ferns that surrounded the orchids tickled her nose. It made her glad that he hadn't seized her gift eagerly, as many people would have done. Nevertheless, she was determined that he was going to take it. 'Please, Rob. I'm just so damned grateful to you for everything you're doing for Mandy. I want you to have a fresh start, and a real place in that practice of yours, as a part-ner——'

'Shauna, I don't want to take this.'

'Why not?' She was irritated. 'It's my money, Rob, and if I want to give you a wedding present——' She looked down at the yellow diamond on her finger. 'I didn't refuse your gift.'

'You tried,' he reminded.

'You didn't listen to me. So I'm not going to listen to you.' She took the cheque from Rob's fingers and slipped it into the inside breast pocket of his navy blazer. 'There,' she said, and straightened his sober rep. tie. 'Don't argue with me.'

Andrea knocked and after a discreet interval put her head in. 'It's time,' she said. 'Jessica finally turned up.'

Shauna bit her lip and slipped her hand into the crook of his arm. Under the soft fabric of his sleeve, his muscles felt taut.

Good, Shauna thought. At least I'm not the only one who's having second thoughts.

They were married in the living-room of the Cohns' townhouse. The guests were few—Jessica; Mandy, who clutched her precious camera but never left Andrea's side; Rob's parents; two of his brothers; a handful of close friends. The rest of Rob's family, he had told her, was scattered across the country, and it would be hard for all of them to attend at such short notice. That's fortunate, Shauna found herself thinking; Andrea simply doesn't have room for any more bodies...

The simple words of the civil ceremony were punctuated by Jessica's tears. 'My little girl,' she announced loudly as soon as the formalities were over. 'Shauna, darling——'

The electronic flash of Mandy's camera went off full in Jessica's eyes, and she broke off to glare at the child.

Shauna removed herself from her mother's embrace as quickly as she could and turned to the tiny woman who was obviously responsible for Rob's blue eyes. How difficult this must be for her, Shauna thought—having to welcome her new daughter-in-law in the middle of a crowd, when she had only just met her. What had been her dreams for Rob? Was there a girl Rob's mother had wanted him to marry? Whatever she had wished for him, certainly it could not have been this kind of haste, Shauna thought. No wonder he had been so reluctant to hurt her any more.

'I don't know what to say, Mrs Stevens,' she began, a little breathlessly.

A smile dawned in the big blue eyes. 'That's your name now, too,' Rob's mother pointed out in a soft Southern accent. 'Why don't we eliminate the confusion? Most everyone in the family just calls me Mum—but my name's Mary if you'd rather use that.'

'I can see why Rob's been keeping you hidden from the rest of the family, Shauna,' his father added. 'He's got a couple of brothers who might try to steal you from him.' His hand nearly engulfed hers, but his grip was gentle and his smile was welcoming.

My God, Shauna thought, my mother had the nerve to insult these people—to imply that Rob's family couldn't possibly be worth knowing—when the truth is I would be proud to be their daughter.

She felt almost ashamed of herself, conscience-stricken at the idea of reducing the sanctity of marriage to a mere legal manoeuvre, when it was so obviously of vital importance to them.

Don't go overboard, she reminded herself. I couldn't have done this alone, and Rob doesn't even have a high principle involved, as I do. He's doing the same thing I am, for money, and he doesn't seem to feel guilty about it, so why should I? But he could at least have warned me——

Andrea's housekeeper had set up a simple buffet in the dining-room, and guests helped themselves and balanced plates where they could; the Cohns' townhouse had not been designed for large-scale entertaining. Mandy was flitting from room to room, too excited by the opportunity to document the occasion on film to have time for things like food.

Shauna couldn't have felt less like eating, herself, but Rob's father insisted on filling a plate for her. She found herself sitting in a corner of the living-room next to a dark-haired young woman who was pleasant enough but very quiet.

'Are you part of Rob's family?' Shauna asked finally. She could see no resemblance, but there was the matter of all those foster kids, and Rob's father had obviously known the girl.

'Oh, no,' the young woman said. 'I'm just a friend.' There was something in the way she said it, though, that sent a prickle of discomfort racing through Shauna's veins. 'I'm a colleague, actually,' the young woman went on. 'Rob and I did our residency together.'

'Oh? Are you in practice in St Louis?'

'I'm working at one of the hospitals here at the moment, but this summer I'm going to the West Coast to start studying again. I'm going to be a specialist in neonatal medicine. Newborns,' she explained unnecessarily.

Shauna smiled sourly. She detested intellectuals who thought no one outside their field knew anything about it.

'Rob had hoped to go on, too, but he didn't have the money.' The young woman looked at Shauna with something like accusation in her eyes. 'It's a sin that he couldn't continue his studies. He's a fantastic doctor, and he ought to be a specialist.' She stopped abruptly and looked down at her plate.

But perhaps Rob has found a way to get his finances in order in a hurry, Shauna thought. Well, it's not as if it's any surprise, that's for sure. I knew that debt was bothering him; it just didn't occur to me to wonder why.

Rob dropped a kiss on Shauna's temple. 'Amy, I'm glad you could come,' he said to the young woman. 'Have you been officially introduced? Amy Evans is the second-best paediatrician in St Louis, Shauna, and one of my all-time favourite women——'

Shauna watched the way colour flickered in the young woman's face, and thought, I wonder if he knows how much she loves him.

'We've been discussing you, as a matter of fact,' she said, and studied his face. Of course he knew, she decided. How could a man be as compassionate, as observant, as brilliant as Rob was, and not know when a woman adored him?

And did he love her, too? Was that why Amy Evans wanted him to come with her? Hadn't he said something that day in the Japanese gardens about having a lot to lose, if this scheme of theirs went astray? Not that it matters, Shauna told herself. Rob had given his word, and she trusted it. Besides, she reflected, a year isn't a long time to wait—not when there's something you want at the end of it. We will all just have to be patient for a year. Then I'll have Mandy, and Rob can do whatever he likes, and this whole thing will not have been in vain.

The housekeeper was gone, of course, when they reached the apartment block, and Mandy was spending the weekend with the Cohns. When they had told her of the plans, Mandy had complained that it was unfair for her to be left out. Andrea had grimaced at Shauna and said, 'I suppose you'd like me to explain marriage to her, too, since the poor child's never seen a real one!'

Walter the doorman stopped them in the lobby to offer his congratulations. But, despite his enthusiastic greeting, Walter seemed a bit bemused, as if he was still trying to make sense of it all. First Mandy moves in, Shauna thought, and now Rob. Walter probably thinks I'll start bringing home stray elephants next . . .

It was late, and the strain of the day had finally dissipated, leaving her exhausted. She fumbled with her key, and Rob held out a hand for it. She gave it up almost reluctantly, which was silly, she told herself. He'd unlocked the door for her several times in the past week. It was just that this time felt so different. This time, he would not be going away——

She didn't even turn on the lights, just kicked off her shoes and sank wearily down on the couch. The glow of the city's lights filtered weakly into the room, silhouetting the furniture. Sitting in the dark and studying the city was one of the things Shauna liked best about her home, but tonight the view didn't attract her.

At least, though, in the dark she didn't have to look at the piles of gifts that nearly filled the dining-room—boxes that had been pouring in all week. There was everything from a china cookie jar, presented in person by a proud Mandy, to an enormous and obviously expensive ceramic and art glass centrepiece from Jessica, to a classically beautiful silver coffee-pot with a note from Rob's parents that explained how it had been passed down in the family for more than two hundred years.

Too bad, Shauna thought, that Mother didn't see that. She would have gone green with envy, but she might have changed her opinion of Rob's family!

'I tried to tell your mother how much I like the coffee-pot,' she said. 'I'll take the best care of it, of course, so when this is over, it can be returned to them——'

He turned abruptly from the window, where he'd been staring out at the black satin surface of the river. But all he said was, 'That's very thoughtful, Shauna.'

Shauna cleared her throat. 'I want you to feel comfortable here,' she ventured carefully, 'but I've got no idea what you'd like. I don't know if you need room for sports equipment or furniture or books. Do you collect things? Besides wild ties and unpaid bills, I mean——'

'The laboratory rats don't take up much space,' he said mildly. 'But they do like privacy, so——'

'Rats?' she repeated hoarsely, and cursed herself for not asking the question a few days sooner. Then she swallowed hard. Make the best of it, Shauna, she ordered herself; that's all you can do, now.

'There is an extra bedroom at the end of the hall that I thought would make a nice office,' she said. 'There's a little desk. I suppose if we took the daybed out you could put cages—— ' She shuddered. And how am I going to explain this, with a no-pets policy in the building? she asked herself.

He sat down beside her. 'Shauna, don't you even know when you're being teased?'

'There aren't any rats?'

He shook his head. 'I got all of that out of my system when I was about ten.'

'Do you mean that your mother actually let you keep rats in her house?'

'No, but I had white mice. They're very clean and awfully interesting, with distinctive personalities——'

She shuddered and buried her face in a cushion.

'All right. I won't tell you about them. Shauna, about that money——'

'I'd rather talk about the mice.' It was muffled, but definite.

Rob sighed. 'You're being completely irrational, you know. What did your father do, anyway, that you've got this kind of pocket money?'

'He picked the right family to be born into. He also had quite a knack with stocks and bonds, I understand. I suppose that's where my liking for finance comes from.'

'You understand? Don't you know?'

'No. He and Mother were divorced when I was six. He pretty much ignored me after that, until he found out he was dying and developed a conscience.'

'Poor Shauna.' Rob's hand brushed against her hair, and she forced herself to stay still under the caress. But his fingers were only seeking out the pins that held the wisp of silk and illusion securely to her head. 'You'll smash your—what do you call this thing, anyway? It's not big enough to be a self-respecting hat.'

Shauna looked at it, cradled in his palm. 'My grand-mother McCoy would have had a fit,' she agreed. 'I don't think she ever went outside her house without her head properly covered.'

'She sounds like an interesting lady.' It was a murmur that invited confidence. 'You've never said much about your family.'

Family matters should stay in the family, Shauna thought. That had been one of many laws learned at her grandmother's knee. 'She wasn't a chocolate-chip-cookie sort of grandmother,' she said softly. 'She saw her duty and she did it—including making sure that I knew how to conduct myself in public. She did it without ever saying a negative word about Mother, too—which, now that I think about it, is pretty amazing.'

'If a lady can't say something good, she says nothing at all?'

'Something like that. She didn't want my father to marry Mother, of course, I know that, and yet I'm quite sure that she never said a word about it to me.'

Rob slipped an arm around her and drew her head down against his shoulder. He had taken his jacket off and loosened his collar. The heavily starched shirt felt slick against Shauna's cheek, and his cologne hinted of spicy musk.

'You lived with your mother after the divorce,' he prompted, 'and she married Sol Abrams——'

She shook her head. 'First she married the jockey. He shot himself after a scandal at the track. Then she married the racing-car driver, but that only lasted six months. After that, she met Sol after a concert he gave here——'

'Goodness.' He kissed the top of her head, gently, and then leaned his cheek against her hair.

'After Sol died, she came back to St Louis, and she stayed single for two whole years. I was actually be ginning to think she meant to go on that way—but then she met Rudy.' She thought it over. 'My mother is a person of eclectic taste. The only thing all of her hus bands had in common was money.' She sighed. 'I like your parents, Rob——'

He chuckled. 'They like you, too. Mum said she could see why I wanted to marry you first, before I let you see the mass confusion that a family reunion at the Stevens' house can be.'

'Family reunion,' Shauna said wistfully. 'That sounds wonderful. What's left of my family could fit in a bathtub.'

'Would you like to go? My father's birthday is in August, and everyone tries to get home for that.'

'I don't know. Wouldn't it be easier for you if I didn't? I mean, if I get involved with your whole family, it's going to be harder for you afterwards——' She thought about it, and said flatly, 'Or maybe it would be a good idea for me to meet them all. They might take one look at me and decide I could never fit in, and then you wouldn't have to explain anything when we file for divorce.'

'That sounds bitter.' He tipped her face up and kissed her lightly. 'They're not ghouls, you know, and we've already got all kinds. You'll fit.'

'That is not a great deal of comfort,' Shauna said. But how nice it would be, she thought, to have a big family. How reassuring it must be to have built-in friendships and unrelenting support. And how very frightening it would be, at the age of twenty-six, to be plunged into that sort of group. 'I've never had a family, really,' she said. 'Just my grandmother, and Mandy.'

'Mandy will love it. She'll have about seventy-three cousins.'

Shauna frowned. She was trying to keep her mind on the conversation, instead of thinking about his fingers, which were drawing tiny, sensual circles on her skin. 'Don't you even know how many there are?'

'You're the accountant,' Rob said cheerfully. 'You can start keeping track. My mother was an only child, but there are all of Dad's brothers and sisters and their kids and grandkids——'

'I don't think I can handle it.'

'In that case, shall we talk about us instead?' It was soft and sultry, and talking was apparently not what was on Rob's mind. His lips brushed against hers, so lightly that it was like the sensual caress of a butterfly's wing, and Shauna felt as if her heart had suddenly begun to stagger drunkenly around inside her. His tongue teased against her lips, and she sagged against him, letting him explore the soft secrets of her mouth. He tasted vaguely like champagne. Her hand crept up to the back of his head, caressing the softness of his hair.

When he released her mouth, she felt almost abandoned for an instant. Then he kissed her eyelids, and said huskily, 'When I came into that room today and you were standing there looking like ice, it was all I could do to keep from dragging you off somewhere and doing this until you looked human again——'

'Why didn't you?' Shauna asked unsteadily.

'Because Andrea told me if I messed up your hair or your make-up, she'd kill me.' His mouth traced a scorching path across her temple to the hollow of her cheek. 'It would have been worth it. I want you so much, Shauna——'

Want. It was as if a bucket of cold water had sloshed over her. He wanted her the same way he wanted food and water, to satisfy a bodily need. It was all she could expect, she told herself, and it would have been infinitely worse if he had said he loved her; it would have been unbearable to listen to the convenient lie. She told herself that she would rather face an unpleasant truth than lull herself with a falsehood. And yet, she thought desperately, if we could only pretend——

We can't pretend for a whole year, she reminded herself. We may as well be honest together.

'I'd like to have a few minutes alone,' she said, in a voice that trembled.

For a moment, she didn't think he'd heard; he seemed reluctant to let her go. Then he said, 'Of course.' He pulled her to her feet and cupped her chin in his hand, raising her face to his. 'It will be all right,' he said, and she nodded, but she was less than certain.

The big bedroom was at least a momentary sanctuary. She closed the door behind her with a sigh, leaned against it, and looked around. This room that she had so carefully made into a refuge and a place of peace was no longer hers alone. In a few minutes, Rob would come in, as he now had every right to do——

My God, she thought. What have I agreed to? A man I've known less than two weeks, and I'm going to go to bed with him. And I always swore I would not be like my mother, that I would not take marriage, and all that goes with it, lightly——

It's far too late to think about it, she told herself.

There was a box on the foot of her bed, a large white box with the embossed mark of the city's most exclusive lingerie shop, The House of Dreams. Louise must have put it there, Shauna thought, but where could it have come from? She opened it warily, and relaxed when she saw Andrea's spiky signature on the card. There was no other message; Andrea, she thought, probably considered that the name of the shop was enough. After the discussion they'd had in front of her on Sunday morning, Andrea could be forgiven for thinking that this marriage might need all the help it could get...

The nightgown was of lace and bronze-coloured satin, low-cut and revealing. The matching négligé was illusion; it was, Shauna thought, mostly a matter of imagination.

She put on the gown and robe and sat down at her dressing-table to brush her hair. Her hands shook so hard that the auburn waves only tangled more.

How different this could have been, she thought. I could be sitting here waiting for Greg to come to me. Instead——

I have agreed, she told herself miserably, to live with, and to sleep with, a man I scarcely recognise. A man who, for all I know, is just as much in love with that young woman doctor as she undoubtedly is with him. A man who only wants to sleep with me because it would be too uncomfortable for him otherwise——

She swept the cosmetics back from the edge of the dressing-table with an unsteady hand, and propped her elbows on the glass, her hands cupping her face.

Rob came in a few minutes later. She was so absorbed in her own thoughts that she did not hear him. She only realised he was there when a gentle hand skimmed over her hair, and then she sat up hurriedly and began to wield her brush frantically.

He took it out of her hand and began to use it himself, long, rhythmic strokes that reduced her tangled hair to glossy waves that fell almost to her waist. She kept her eyes closed; she could not bear to look into the mirror and see his reflection there, instead of the face of the man she loved.

He laid the brush aside and stooped over her, gathering up the long, fragrant strands of hair so he could kiss the hidden spot at the nape of her neck. Her skin quivered under the pressure of his lips as he caressed the silky triangle under her ear, tugging gently at the tiny lobe with his teeth, and then turning his attention to the hollow at the base of her throat where her pulse beat jerkily.

'I can't,' she said hoarsely.

For a moment, he was absolutely still, his mouth pressed against her throat. 'I thought we'd agreed to be sensible about this,' he said.

'We did,' Shauna admitted. 'But I just—can't.' Her voice trailed off into a miserable quaver.

He pulled back, then. Amazingly enough, she realised, he didn't look angry, just curious. 'Too many memories?' he said gently.

'Perhaps——' She swallowed hard. 'Perhaps the problem is that I have too few memories.'

He frowned. 'I think I'd like to hear about this fiancé of yours.'

'What's Greg got to do with this?'

'Obviously more than you want to talk about. Look, I can understand if he was so special that you don't want to make love with anyone else. I am not completely insensitive, and actually I prefer having a lady's attention all on me, and not on her former lover. But if you loved him so damned much, Shauna, why drag me into it? Why didn't you go talk to him when you decided you had to have a husband?'

'I couldn't.'

'He jilted you?'

'Of course not! I'm the one who broke——' She stopped abruptly.

'Then I'm afraid I don't understand. You didn't want to marry him; you did want to marry me. You don't want to make love with me, and yet you swore it was all over with him——'

'It is.'

'Then I'm damned if I understand what you're talking about.'

'Rob, I've never——' Her voice broke. 'I've never made love with anyone, and——'

He looked at her in blank astonishment. 'You told me you were taking the pill,' he reminded harshly.

'I am. But you didn't let me explain it. I have a very irregular cycle—it was the easiest way to——'

'That's certainly handy.'

'Dammit, Rob, I'm not lying to you! You can call my doctor if you want!'

He gave a shout of laughter. 'I can see his face, if I get him out of bed at this hour to consult about my wife's medical history. No, don't try to explain it, Shauna. I did my time in gynaecology. Isn't that just my luck? I've discovered the only twenty-six-year-old virgin in the Western Hemisphere——'

'That is not funny.' She thought better of the sharp tone, and added, 'I know this is an awful thing to do——'

'Honey, you have no idea.' He threw himself down on her bed.

'I wasn't going to tell you,' she ventured uncertainly. 'I really intended to keep my word, Rob——'

'Give me a little credit,' he muttered. 'Before we went too much further, I would have guessed.'

He had thrown an arm across his face, and for a long moment he didn't move. In fact, Shauna began to wonder if he had gone to sleep, but surely, she thought, that just wasn't possible.

Finally, he sighed and sat up. 'Obviously,' he said, 'the gentlemanly thing for me to do is to take a cold shower and go to another room. And fortunately for you, Shauna, my mother taught me never to take advantage of a lady.'

'I'll send her a thank-you note,' Shauna said under her breath.

'Whether a real lady would treat a man this way is open for discussion,' he went on, 'but I'll give you the benefit of the doubt for tonight.'

She felt as if she had been slapped. But it was no wonder he was being sarcastic, Shauna told herself. She deserved it, every cutting word of it. She was a tease, and worse. She, who prided herself on her honesty and trustworthiness, had gone back on her word, and it made her feel like a rat. And what if his answer was that her broken promise invalidated their entire arrangement? She couldn't blame him, that was sure. He'd made very plain what he expected, and now she was reneging on the deal...

She watched him in the mirror as he walked to the door. He turned with his hand on the knob. 'If you change your mind again, Shauna,' he said, 'do me a favour and put it in writing.'

She whispered in relief, 'Thank you for understanding.'

'Don't kid yourself,' he warned. 'I certainly didn't say that I understood. Believe me, Shauna, this is not over—and as I warned you once, under these conditions it could be a very long year for us both.'

The door closed behind him with a quiet swoosh that was more final than a slam. She sat there for a long time in silence, and then she put her head down on the dressing-table and sobbed until her throat ached and her eyes burned and the bronze satin gown was permanently stained with her tears.

CHAPTER SEVEN

THE days were growing longer, Shauna realised as she wiped off the kitchen counter and rinsed the dishcloth out. She stood by the window and looked across the city towards the sunset sky. April had crept into May. The dogwood trees that had spattered the landscape with lacy white had dropped their veils of blossoms now and receded into the surrounding green for another year. Azaleas had given way to lilac. That was one thing she missed by living downtown; there was no place to dig in the earth here, and there were few growing things to mark the passing seasons.

'You are becoming positively domestic,' she muttered.

'Are you talking to yourself?' Mandy demanded from her seat at the kitchen table.

'Yes. They tell me that it's a symptom of parenthood. If you're finished with your dinner, the piano is waiting for you.'

'Can I take violin lessons next year instead?'

'Possibly. But that isn't going to get you out of practising tonight.'

Mandy scowled, but she obediently cleared away her dirty dishes and went off towards the living-room. A few minutes later the first strains of a Chopin étude split the air with a discord the composer had certainly never intended, and Shauna winced.

It isn't that Mandy's a bad kid, she told herself. And some day, she will appreciate the fact that she learned to play. I hope.

She loaded the dishwasher and started it, and then checked the refrigerator. The housekeeper had left steaks tonight. That was easy enough. As soon as Rob got home, whenever that was, she'd start them broiling. It was apt to be a while; he was never out of the office on time. No wonder the senior doctors had offered him a partnership, she reflected. They knew a good man when they saw one.

She wondered if he'd made up his mind yet about whether to accept their offer. Perhaps he had decided just to stay one more year as an employee, and then go back to school. He had the money, now, and even though she hadn't intended it to be used quite that way, she would certainly understand. Perhaps I should talk to him about that when he gets home, she thought.

In the meantime, she'd have a little time to herself, as long as she kept one ear tuned to the piano practice. Long enough to wash her hair and start a manicure. It amazed her sometimes that the new demands on her evening hours didn't bother her more, but perhaps she had lived alone so long that it was a relief to have people around.

It had been just a little more than two weeks since the wedding, and they had already fallen into a pattern. At least Shauna had; there was no predicting Rob's schedule. The man worked phenomenal hours——

Or perhaps it would be more accurate to say that he was gone long hours, Shauna told herself. There was no point in lying to herself about it, and as far as that went, she didn't blame him. 'I'd much rather he be playing tennis or racquetball after office hours than hanging about the apartment and trying to seduce me,' she muttered. And as far as anything else he might be doing— well, she had asked for it when she had backed out of their agreement.

Not that he had tried to change her mind, after the fiasco of their wedding night. In fact, he'd been leaving her strictly alone. He treated her much as a big brother would—just about the same way he treated Mandy. He even came into her bedroom each evening to say good-night and brush her hair——

At first she had been startled, almost panicked, about those nightly visits. But all he did was brush her hair till it fell in a gleaming river about her shoulders, then kiss the nape of her neck and go away as quietly as he had come. So she didn't worry about it any more.

To be perfectly honest, she reflected, the hair-brushing bothered her less than some other things he did. The first time he had come in from playing tennis, for instance, still hot from the exercise, his shirt wet and a towel draped around his neck, had been a revelation. Shauna had never before realised that honest sweat was as attractive a scent as the most expensive cologne, but she had learned it that day when he stopped to give her a casual kiss on his way to the shower. She had watched him walk away from her down the hall, easy grace in his long stride, and she had coloured in embarrassment when she realised that it was almost a hungry appraisal that she was making, a survey that took careful note of lean hips and well-muscled long legs . . .

After that, when he played tennis, she had made it a point not to be in the living-room when he came home. But it didn't erase the awareness of him that had started that day in the Japanese garden as they stood on the zigzag bridge.

For the first time she admitted that it hadn't been very comfortable around the flat since Rob had moved in. She hadn't expected that it would bother her, but she had to admit that she felt increasingly guilty about backing out of her promise. The growing tension was making her miserable, but Rob seemed to be taking it in his stride, and she kept telling herself that she was being silly about the whole thing. It would only have complicated an already difficult situation if he had insisted on sharing her bed, and she was glad that he was being reasonable about it. It was much, much better to leave things as they were.

But she wondered sometimes, as she lay awake and watched the moonlight filter through the lacy curtains in her bedroom, just why it didn't seem to bother him. Was he spending those extra, unaccounted-for hours with someone else? Amy Evans would be willing, she was sure of that . . .

She heard the front door open, and she glanced at the kitchen clock, startled. She hadn't expected him for another hour at least.

She grimaced. When he's gone, she told herself, you're wondering where he is. And when he comes home, you wish he'd stay away. Why don't you make up your mind, Shauna? What is it you want?

There was a murmur of voices in the living-room, and then the Chopin étude started up again. The notes flowed smoothly and gently, each one precise and perfect. It obviously wasn't a professional at the keyboard, but it was quite pleasant.

Shauna was standing in the centre of the kitchen with her mouth open in astonishment when Rob came in. 'What did you do to Mandy?' she demanded. 'Wave a magic wand? She's been struggling with that music for half an hour——'

Rob reached into the refrigerator for a can of ginger ale. 'I didn't do anything much. I just pointed out that it would be easier to play it right than it was to butcher it on purpose.'

'She's been making that awful noise intentionally?'

'Hadn't you noticed? Her sense of rhythm is perfect, and she's quite capable of playing the notes. Therefore, when the piece keeps getting worse instead of better, the only possible conclusion is that she's doing it on purpose. Listen to her, Shauna—I think you'll recognise some jazz in there.'

'Do you read minds, too?' Shauna handed him a glass.

'And palms. But only at school carnivals.' The usual bantering note was missing from his voice.

Shauna looked at him suspiciously. He looked very tired, she thought. There were more fine lines around his eyes than usual, as if he was trying to retreat from something he didn't want to see. He'd been on call the night before, and the telephone had rung several times in the small hours of the morning. She knew because no matter how quick he was to answer it, the extension phone ringing beside her bed usually roused her anyway.

'I'm broiling steaks tonight,' she said. 'Mandy has already had her dinner. Do you want to eat now or wait a while?'

He sat down at the table and poured his ginger ale into the glass. 'I'm not hungry.'

'I thought you were going to play racquetball tonight.'

'I didn't feel like it.'

'I'm not surprised, after the night you had. I heard you go out about three.' He hadn't come back; the breakfast table had been awfully quiet with only Mandy and Shauna there. It was funny, she thought, how quickly I've grown to miss him when he's gone.

'I didn't mean to wake you. And I'm sorry I couldn't take Mandy to school this morning.'

'For heaven's sake, Rob, you take her every day. It certainly didn't bother me to do it once.' She poured herself a glass of sparkling water. 'Rob,' she added hesitantly, 'have you decided anything about your partnership in the practice yet?'

He shook his head. 'What's this?' he asked, turning over an envelope on the kitchen table.

Something was wrong, she thought. Badly wrong. But he obviously didn't want to talk about it, and she certainly couldn't force him. 'Mandy's photographs from the wedding came back from the developer today. She's been chortling over them all afternoon.'

He was flipping through the brightly coloured bits of paper. 'She has more enthusiasm than skill, I see,' he mused.

'Oh, I don't know. There's a rather wonderful shot of Mother with her mouth wide open.' She spread the pictures out. 'Here.' There were other photographs in the bunch that Shauna would just as soon ignore—like the one of her sitting beside Amy Evans, with Rob bending over them. I looked like a hag that day, she thought. I looked so awful on my wedding day, it's a wonder no one seemed to see through to the truth...

'Quite a souvenir,' Rob said. He picked up a picture of the two of them. It showed most of Shauna's orchid bouquet, but the top of Rob's head was missing.

'And she got two copies of everything, so we can have a full set. Thoughtful of her, wasn't it?' Shauna's tone was ironic.

'We could have a ceremonial burning. But that would hurt Mandy's feelings.' He held up a blurry photo of someone who might have been his mother, and then put it down with a sigh. 'Besides, some day these will be hysterically funny.'

'To whom?' It was tart, and only after the words were out did Shauna really think about it. Would she look at these some day, alone, and laugh? Somehow, she doubted it. By the time this year was over, she would be glad to put all the reminders away.

'Trust me. Your mother might enjoy them.'

'Not the one of her. If she decides she wants Mandy back next year, all we have to do is threaten to publish it.' She pushed the photographs back into a pile, with one of Richard and Andrea on top. Richard was looking old all of a sudden, she thought sadly. 'Speaking of Mother,' she added, 'I got a letter from her this morning.'

'Oh? How does she like *hacienda* living?'

'Not much. It was six pages of self-pitying laments. Mother's not speaking to Rudy because he didn't tell her that all the movie people would be living with them in the *hacienda*. I don't think she'd mind if it was just the stars, but even the lowliest camera assistant agrees with her that the village is uninhabitable. And I was right about the exterminator, too—she says the bugs are as big as limousines and nearly as fast. If we don't hear from her again, we're to assume that one of them has carried her off.'

'One of the insects? Or one of the movie people?'

'From her letter, I'm not sure she thinks there's a difference.'

Rob smiled, but it didn't quite reach his eyes.

'Did you have any sleep at all last night?' Shauna asked gently.

'Not much. I had a nap in the doctors' lounge.'

'Why don't you rest before dinner?'

'I might.' He got up, wearily, and ran a hand through his hair.

'I'll wait until you wake up before I start the steaks,' Shauna offered. 'Rob——'

He paused in the doorway.

'If you want to talk about it——' she offered hesitantly.

He shook his head. 'Thanks, honey, but it's something I have to work out for myself.'

That's it, then, she told herself. She could do nothing about it.

But she wondered, a little guiltily, if it was the partnership that was nagging at him, or something else. This kind of thing wasn't like Rob—the straightforward man who made up his mind and didn't hesitate to say what he thought. If he didn't want to talk about this—whatever it was—with her, did that mean it concerned her, and he didn't want to say anything until he'd decided what to do?

He apparently didn't take a nap. There was a light under his tightly closed door when she came out of

Mandy's room after kissing her goodnight, and she stood thoughtfully in the hall for a moment and then tapped lightly. 'Rob?' she said softly.

His desk chair creaked. 'Come in.'

'Mandy wants you to come and say goodnight.' His desk blotter was covered with books, she saw. They were piled atop of one another as if he was searching for something, and he hadn't even looked up from the page when she opened the door. 'I'll start the steaks now,' she said.

'Don't bother. I don't want anything.'

'Rob, you have to eat——' Then she thought better of it. He wasn't a child, after all, and she wasn't his mother. 'All right. If you get hungry later, there's plenty of stuff in the refrigerator.'

She took a shower and did her nails. It's not your problem, Shauna, she told herself, but that didn't help to erase her concern. When for the first time in two weeks he didn't come to brush her hair, her apprehension grew. Whatever it was, she was quite sure by now that it involved her, and she didn't like the idea of sitting by quietly and waiting while he made up his mind.

Finally, when the light under his door was still glowing at midnight, she found herself standing in the hallway. At least I can say goodnight, she thought. Maybe he'll tell me what he's thinking.

He was lying across the brass-railed daybed, face down, when she peeped in. He hadn't bothered to undress or turn down the bed; the chintz spread was rumpled. On the desk, the lamp still burned, and the pile of books had grown larger. They were medical texts, she saw. It made her feel a little better, for a moment, until she realised that his books might be the way he worked out all frustrations. How very little she really knew about him, she thought. She only knew how much it bothered her when he was unhappy.

'Rob?' she whispered. 'I wanted to say good-night——' She put a hand on his shoulder and was shocked at the tension she could feel in his muscles.

He obviously hadn't heard her come in. When she touched him, he sat up with a jerk, ran his hand across his jaw, and said, 'I forgot the time——'

'I thought you might have.' Her hand was still on his shoulder; she could feel a sort of flicker in the muscle as the warmth of her palm soothed him a little. 'Rob?' she whispered. 'Are you angry with me?'

He looked startled. Then he smiled and ruffled her hair, which was hanging loose around her shoulders. 'No, Shauna. I'm sorry I've been a bear—I'll be all right tomorrow.'

'Not if you don't get some sleep. And as tense as you are...' She let her fingers creep across to the base of his neck; the muscles there were just as tight. 'Take your shirt off. I'll be right back.'

His eyebrows went up. 'Is this some sort of invitation?'

Shauna's cheeks coloured a little, but she kept her voice steady. 'No, it's an order.'

When she came back a moment later with a bottle of body lotion, he was sitting on the edge of the bed. He eyed the bottle warily, but obeyed when she told him to stretch out on his stomach. 'This has sort of a feminine scent to it,' she warned, 'but it's the only thing I've got.'

'Are you going to pour that stuff on me?' he wanted to know. 'Because if it's cold, I'm likely to go straight through the ceiling——'

'It won't be cold when I get done with it.' She folded her yellow kimono around her and sat down on the edge of the bed. She poured lotion into her palm and warmed it between her hands.

He propped himself up on his elbows and sniffed. 'What is the name of that stuff?'

'It's the same scent as my perfume, and you don't want to know what it's called.' She pushed him down and began to rub his neck and shoulders, her fingers digging gently into the muscles, the friction warming and relaxing them.

He sighed a little, and turned his face into a pillow. 'It's still cold,' he said, his voice muffled. 'But I'll forgive you. Who taught you to give back rubs?'

'A nurse I had when I was little.'

'You may regret letting me in on the secret, you know.' Then he fell silent.

After a few minutes, she said, 'Did you lose a special child today?'

'Am I that transparent?'

'No. But I'm not dumb, either.' Her hands never stopped moving, massaging with gentle force. 'Give me a little credit. If it isn't me, then it must be something that happened earlier today, and I suspect it was probably a patient. If there was anything you could do, you'd be at the hospital doing it. Instead, you're reading at home——' She stopped, knowing that she was trespassing on private territory. And perhaps it didn't matter if he told her, after all, she thought; there was comfort just in knowing that right now he needed her.

He sighed. 'I haven't lost him yet,' he said. 'But I'm afraid I'm going to. He's four years old, and he's one of the neatest kids I've ever treated, Shauna. I've changed his medications again, and I'm hoping he'll respond. So far, nothing has made any difference at all. There's so little we can do, and so many things we don't know——'

Her heart ached for him, and for the parents who might lose their child. What if it was Mandy? she thought. 'Does it happen often?' she asked softly.

'Too damned often. Some of them are harder than others. And no matter how many, you never get used to it.' For a moment, he sounded bitter, and almost defeated.

'Of course you don't,' Shauna whispered. 'If you did, you wouldn't be the doctor—and the man—that you are.' She pressed her lips gently against the smooth brown skin of his shoulderblade. He didn't move or speak, and she flushed just a little with embarrassment at being so openly sentimental, and went back to gently rubbing his back, massaging each separate muscle, kneading his spine, until the last bit of tension was gone, and his breathing was deep and regular.

It might be sentimental, but it was true, she told herself. He was a very special doctor, a very special man. She knew instinctively that he was careful never to allow himself to become so personally involved that his professional judgement would be at risk, and yet each child had a special piece of his heart. When one didn't make it, Rob would grieve, and then he would try his best to make sure that it never happened again.

He was asleep, she thought, and was suddenly, fiercely glad that she had come in to say goodnight. She wished that he hadn't gone to sleep in his clothes, but surely it would be better to leave him that way than to wake him. Any rest at all would be welcome.

She shifted her weight off the mattress as slowly as she could, willing it not to move and disturb him. She stood and looked down at him for a long moment, and then turned towards the door, intending to get a blanket from her own room to cover him.

His voice followed her, low, husky. 'Shauna——'

Her kimono belt slipped a fraction as she swung around, and the neckline deepened to display the creamy shadow between her breasts.

'My God,' he said, 'you're so beautiful, with the light glowing through your hair——'

She tightened the belt absently, her eyes on him as he came towards her. His trousers were wrinkled, his hair rumpled, but she thought that she had never seen him looking more attractive.

If was a brief and gentle kiss that he placed on her lips; a sort of thank-you, she thought. At least, it started out to be that way. But there was a single moment when she looked up at him, her head thrown back, her lips parted, her breath coming quickly—a moment that seemed to stretch out into an eon, and she knew that she wanted it to be much more than that.

You made a promise, Shauna, she told herself, not only to Rob but to yourself. You can keep that promise now, or you can back away. If there ever was a time to be honest with yourself about what it is you want, this is it . . .

Desire, he had said, is a trap either of us could be caught in, and he had been right. She did desire him— she had been doing so for days—and that feeling wasn't going to go away. Why frustrate them both for the next year, when what they wanted was the same? It was so very simple, after all.

She saw the question in his eyes, and she raised a hand to gently follow the outline of his jaw. Her fingers seemed to wander of their own accord to a wayward lock of hair, and then to the back of his head, pulling his face down to hers——

He let her go a few moments later, with a groan. She tried to pull him back, but he held her a little away from him, with his palms cupping her face. 'Shauna, this is torture,' he said. 'Being here—having you in my arms— you don't know what it does to me.'

'I know what it does to me,' she whispered, with painful honesty.

'Then have pity on me. And don't play with fire—my resistance is low, and I'm likely to drag you back in here and rape you. There are limits——'

She felt a moment's compunction. She had been thinking only of herself, and what she wanted. 'You're right,' she whispered, 'You're so tired, and it's so late...'

For the space of a breath she actually meant it, and then she knew that this had gone too far, that neither of them would rest tonight even if she went to her room right now.

'I lose a lot more sleep over you than I do when I'm on call,' Rob admitted huskily.

She looked over his shoulder at the narrow daybed, and then she very deliberately stepped closer to him, fitting herself against his body, letting the silk of the kimono slide sensually against his bare chest. The friction of the fabric against her skin seemed to raise the temperature of her blood, and through its thinness she could feel the urgency of his body and the way his heart was pounding, so strongly that it seemed her breasts would be bruised by its hammering.

'What does it matter if I lose a little more?' he whispered. His arms closed tightly around her, pressing her even more closely against him, until she thought that she would never be able to breathe again. 'I want so much to make love to you that I ache,' he said.

She smiled up at him—a madonna smile—and pushed him a fraction of an inch away. 'I know,' she murmured. 'But not here. Come to bed, Rob——'

She had left both bedside lamps on in her room; she didn't usually do that, and she wondered, just a little, if she had planned this in some half-conscious way. But she put that out of her mind as she moved about the bedroom, folding the blankets back with more precision than she usually bothered with, fluffing the pillows, turning down the lights. Then she shrugged out of the kimono—it made a butter-coloured pool where it fell in the middle of the carpet—and slipped between the satin sheets beside him.

Rob drew her down to him, her hair falling in a sort of curtain around them both, shutting out the world. Her breasts brushed against his chest, and the sensitive nipples contracted eagerly. His eyes were dark with passion; suddenly shy, she buried her face against his shoulder, and wrinkled her nose at the overpowering scent of body lotion.

He laughed, ruefully. 'You've got no one to blame but yourself, Shauna,' he pointed out. 'I must smell as if I've just come from a high-class whorehouse.'

'Does that mean you don't like my perfume?'

'On you, it smells great. Especially when you wear it here, or here——' He kissed the hollow at the base of her throat, and Shauna shivered. His lips wandered down to her breast, and he began to play with her nipple, drawing it gently into his mouth. His hands almost spanned her narrow waist, and his thumbs traced slow, sensual circles on her soft skin.

'Rob——' she said breathlessly. But just then all the glorious sensations he was arousing seemed to coalesce into one. It became a throbbing hunger that demanded satisfaction, and she forgot what she had intended to ask. This time when she said his name it was almost a pleading sob, and he moved above her and then inside her, gently, swiftly, surely. She cried out once in surprised pleasure, and she arched against him, and then it seemed that there was no longer his body and hers. They were one being, merged together into a dance as old and as timeless as the world itself, and nothing else could possibly matter any more, nothing but the incredible torrent building inside her, until every cell seemed to shatter in a simultaneous burst of excruciating, ecstatic splendour...

A little later, when she could move again, she turned her head and looked into his eyes. They were blue once more, she thought hazily, but a different blue than she had ever seen before—a dusky, sultry colour that made no effort to conceal the aftermath of passion.

'Oh,' she said. It was a soft croak.

'Shauna?' It was hesitant, quiet. 'I'm sorry if I hurt you. I didn't mean to——'

She shook her head. 'So that's why you didn't like the idea of a marriage of convenience.'

He grinned, and traced the fragile line of her ear with the tip of his tongue. 'That's why.'

'I quite understand,' she said. 'But I still have one question.'

He raised his head enquiringly. He looked a little apprehensive, she thought. 'What?'

'Rob, how do you know how a high-class whorehouse smells?'

For an instant he was absolutely still. Then he rolled abruptly on to his back, and Shauna found herself sprawled across him, both her wrists clasped tight in one of his hands and held against the pillow above his head. She was completely helpless, made prisoner by her own weight, and the more she twisted about in an effort to escape, the more aware she became that they had not exhausted the passion that flared between them. They had only started to explore...

She stopped fighting. He released her hands, and she nestled them under his head. Her hair swept across his face, and he played with a lock of it and said, 'Do you always wear your hair up when you're in public?'

She nodded.

He smiled, and kissed her, 'Good,' he whispered. 'Because when it's down, it's too intimate, and altogether too sexy, for you to be let loose on the world——' Then his fingers tangled in the length of it, and pulled her down to him again.

CHAPTER EIGHT

IT WAS still grey dawn when Shauna woke. For a moment, she lay still, quietly hugging to herself the delightful memories of the night. But when she turned to share her joy with Rob, he was gone. Only a dent in the pillow and the disarranged blankets confirmed that he had been beside her at all—that, and the knowledge deep inside her that her world had been readjusted somehow, to a slightly different orbit.

She wasn't angry that he hadn't stayed beside her; she knew that he was probably back at that child's bedside. But she was sad that he had crept out without letting her know he was going. He could at least have kissed me goodbye, she thought. I wouldn't have minded if he'd woken me up.

She turned over, and the slickness of the satin sheet gliding across her skin rekindled the sensual memories of the night. It was an almost physical pain.

But it was a very different sort of pain from the one she had been feeling since the wedding. That pain, she admitted now, had been at least partly a growing curiosity about what it would be like if he made love to her. And now she knew.

If she had stopped to reason it out logically before things had exploded last night, she decided, she would probably have concluded that sleeping with Rob was the only sensible, rational thing to do. She might have persuaded herself that, once the mystery was gone, the uncomfortable awareness she felt each time she saw him would recede, and they could live compatibly under a single roof in peace.

But she hadn't been logical about it, of course; she had acted purely on impulse last night. And just as well, too, she told herself, for she could see now that the logical approach was sheer stupidity, mixed with a good dose of naïve reasoning. Sleeping with Rob hadn't erased anything; it had only awakened new longings and new desires——

And I'm not the only one who felt them, she reminded herself. A peaceful smile tugged at her lips, as she remembered.

'You look pleased with yourself.'

Shauna sat up with a start. He closed the door quietly and came towards the bed. He was wearing a terry robe the same dark blue as his eyes.

The sheet slid and she made a futile grab for it. Then, when she saw the interest in Rob's eyes, and the answering colour began to rise in her face, she forgot about things like modesty. What did that matter any more? He was her husband, after all, and the sight of her certainly didn't seem to displease him . . .

'I thought you'd gone already.' She reached for the extra pillows piled by the side of the bed, and began to stack them against the quilted headboard.

'Only to call the hospital.' He handed the rest of the pillows to her, then sat down on the edge of the bed.

She looked up at him with apprehension in her face, but he was smiling. 'He's better, Shauna. He's responding to the change of treatment I ordered last night. I think he's going to make it.'

Shauna flung her arms around him. It was an innocent, congratulatory hug. 'I'm glad,' she whispered.

'And what about us, Shauna?' he asked, very softly. 'When you woke this morning, were you glad that I was gone?'

She didn't quite know what to say. What could she tell him, anyway, that she hadn't already said last night with her body? Surely he couldn't think that anything could possibly have changed how she felt, in these few brief hours——

She shook her head; a stray lock of hair dropped over her shoulder and curled enticingly around the curve of her breast. Rob stroked the auburn strands with a gentle finger, and Shauna looked up at him and licked her lips.

She honestly wasn't trying to be seductive, and when Rob groaned as if he was in pain she was startled. He pushed her back into the nest of pillows and began to kiss her with a sure hunger that made her body ache for him. She tugged the terry robe down off his shoulders and then flung it aside and locked her fingers together at the back of his neck. But there was no need to hold him; their shared passion had them both in its grip, and there was no escape, short of the ultimate release they sought together...

Rob kissed her goodbye at the breakfast table, mischievously choosing a moment when Shauna was just setting her coffee-cup down. His tongue darted briefly between her lips; the cup rattled and coffee slopped into the saucer, and Mandy said, with concern, 'Don't you like to be kissed, Shauna?'

'It just startled me,' Shauna said. She hadn't quite got her voice back.

'But Rob always kisses you goodbye.'

'Yes, dear.' She looked up at Rob, and muttered, 'But not always like that!'

'You object?' he asked innocently.

'I'll get even.' It was an idle threat.

He grinned. 'Oh, that sounds promising.'

Mandy just looked confused.

After they left, Shauna finished her coffee in leisure, staring out of the dining-room window and smiling to herself now and then.

The housekeeper came in a few minutes later. 'Is there anything special you'd like me to pick up when I shop?'

'I can't think of anything, Louise.' Shauna pushed her cup aside. 'There is one thing you could do today, though, if you have time,' she said. She didn't look at the housekeeper. 'Would you move Dr Stevens's clothes from the blue room into my bedroom, please? You can clear the winter things out of my cupboards to make space.'

'Well,' said the housekeeper. There was a world of meaning in the single word. 'No wonder you and Doctor Rob didn't eat those steaks last night. I thought maybe he didn't like steak.'

'I'm sure the steaks were fine. It was just that——' Shauna bit her tongue. The last thing she needed to do was start explaining herself to the housekeeper!

'You'd better start feeding that man right,' Louise advised. 'It might not make any difference just now, but I can guarantee you that if you don't, you'll be sorry——'

Shauna reached for her briefcase and her linen jacket. 'Louise, just move the clothes.'

'Yes, ma'am.' But Louise was grinning.

Shauna was still doing her daily review of Mandy's trust fund when her secretary told her that Andrea Cohn was in the outer office. Andrea knew that this hour of the day was always reserved for Shauna's private work, and she often stopped by if she needed something in a hurry. Shauna shuffled the papers back into Mandy's folder and looked up with a smile as the door opened.

Andrea was carrying a pink box, embossed in silver with the name of the most prestigious department store in St Louis. 'This was just delivered for you,' she said, and set it on Shauna's blotter. 'Susan wasn't quite sure what to do with it. What have you been buying, anyway—perfume by the gallon?'

Shauna was startled. 'I haven't shopped at that store in months.'

Andrea shrugged. 'So maybe they're trying to lure you back.'

Shauna untied the silver cord and cautiously lifted the lid. Nestled atop the pink tissue paper was a card. She read it and turned the colour of the box.

'From an admirer, obviously,' Andrea said drily.

'It's from Rob.' She pushed the tissue paper aside.

'Well, that's much nicer than buying it yourself. It is perfume, isn't it? Are you still using Midnight Passion?'

'Yes, I am. But it doesn't look like that kind of bottle.' And how Rob could have found out the name of her brand was more than she could guess, unless he'd been snooping on her dressing-table, and he'd had other things on his mind this morning... She started to feel a little wobbly, just thinking about what he'd had on his mind. Back to business, Shauna, she told herself firmly.

Of course, she thought. The department store would have a record of her purchases. I shouldn't even peep, with Andrea here, she thought. It could be nearly anything, coming from Rob. But it was driving her crazy not to know. Getting flowers from him this morning wouldn't have surprised her a bit, but this——

She pushed the tissue paper gingerly aside and pulled a plastic bottle out of the box.

'Body lotion?' Andrea said, on a note of disbelief. 'Ordinary, old-fashioned, unscented body lotion? What is the matter with the man? I thought he specialised in romantic gestures——'

Shauna giggled. Now it made sense. She retrieved the card and slipped it into the most secure pocket of her attaché case, just so she didn't have to explain it.

'Next time,' Rob had written, 'I'd rather have my Midnight Passion smelling only of you.'

'Private joke,' Shauna said, with a shrug.

'I should say.' Andrea leaned back in the leather chair and watched her thoughtfully. 'How's Mandy?'

'She's fine. The stomach-aches seem to be a thing of the past.' She nestled the bottle back into the box with a smile.

'I'm glad. All your efforts have paid off.' It sounded as though Andrea would like to say more, and was restraining herself with an effort.

'You could say that,' Shauna murmured. She tied the silver band around the box.

'If you've finished playing with that,' Andrea said drily, 'I've got a client I'd like to talk to you about. It's a divorce case, and I'm having a heck of a time figuring out where all the assets have gone. I thought perhaps you could put me on track.'

They were nearly finished when Shauna's secretary buzzed her on the intercom. 'Dr Stevens is on the telephone,' she said. 'Shall I tell him you'll call back?'

'No, thanks, Susan, I'll take it. I hope you don't mind, Andrea—I'll just be a minute, and Rob's so busy with patients that it's very hard for me to catch him.'

Andrea shrugged and turned back to the paperwork that covered Shauna's desk.

'I'm having a difficult morning,' Rob announced. 'That damned lotion must have soaked clear through me—I thought I had it all scrubbed off, but every time my office nurse walks past me she makes a funny face——'

Shauna giggled. 'It's only your imagination, Rob.'

'In any case, that isn't what I called about. It's my afternoon off, and it actually looks as if I'll get out of here on time.'

'Are you going home for a nap?'

'Only if you'll join me.'

'That wouldn't be very restful.'

'Is that a promise?' It was a sexy murmur.

'I have a very busy afternoon, Rob.'

'I'd really like to talk to you, Shauna.' He sounded disappointed, and the playfulness was gone from his voice. 'Can't you manage to get out of there a little early?'

'Rob, I——' She reached for her list of appointments. That client could be shifted; another was not particularly important—— That's not true, Shauna, she told herself. It's just that you'd much rather be with Rob, and if he can take the afternoon off, so can you.

'All right. I'll work something out.' She put the telephone down and stared thoughtfully at the page of her appointment book. Then she buzzed her secretary. 'Susan, cancel my appointments for this afternoon.'

There was a moment of confused silence in the outer office. 'Did you say *cancel* them, Mrs Stevens?' the secretary asked, as if she thought her hearing might have suddenly gone on the blink.

'And please try to keep my Tuesday afternoons free from now on. I think I'll be out of the office a little more often.' She turned back to Andrea, who was watching open-mouthed. 'We still need some information on those tax shelters, but I think I can get that from my broker——'

Andrea interrupted. 'Shauna,' she said. 'I've known you for ever, and I've watched and applauded in the last three years as you've convinced the business community in this city that you were serious about your profession, not just a little rich girl who would take any excuse to avoid working. You work longer and harder hours than any other accountant I know. I've seen you turn down lunch dates with Greg——'

'Greg?' Shauna said, as if she didn't recognise the name.

'—and golf matches and trips out of town because it would interfere with your work——'

'That's right. And now that I've established myself, I'm going to take life a bit easier.' It was cool.

Andrea said flatly, 'There is certainly nothing wrong with that. But you sound like a woman who's head over heels——'

'In love? Don't be ridiculous.'

'You're infatuated, then, and that's even worse.'

'Andrea, please. You're not my mother——'

'No, but I'm your lawyer, and I have every reason to be concerned.'

'If you'd like,' Shauna said with acid sweetness, 'I'll frame my marriage certificate and hang it by my front door. Andrea, for heaven's sake, I'm——'

'If you're going to frame things,' Andrea said, 'perhaps you should include the pre-nuptial contract you signed.' She started to stack the papers. 'And don't forget, Shauna, that your arrangement with Rob is only for a year.'

'I haven't forgotten anything.'

Andrea slipped the problem papers back into her briefcase. The silence dragged out, and finally she looked up with regret in her eyes. 'Darling, forgive me,' she said. 'It's none of my business. But I just can't stand to see you hurt, and I'm afraid for you. Don't let yourself be trapped, Shauna——'

'I thought you said you liked Rob.' Shauna hardly recognised her own voice.

'I do, and there is nothing I'd like better than to see you happily married. But this isn't a marriage, it's a business deal, and I'm afraid you've forgotten there's a difference. I'm scared that Rob is only using you. Shauna, that was a great deal of money you paid out to take care of his debts. And all he promised was a year.'

'That's all I asked of him.'

'And what if you had asked more?'

There was no answer to that; Amy Evans's dark little face flashed into Shauna's mind, and she remembered what the woman had said. *I'm going to the West Coast...*

Rob had hoped to continue his training, too... It's a sin that he couldn't...

Well, now he could.

Andrea was right, she thought. Rob would not have promised more than a year, because he had no intention of staying in St Louis. If he had really wanted to join that practice, he would have done it by now, she realised; it had been two full weeks since she had given him the money to do so. Was that what he wanted to talk to her about this afternoon? Was he going to remind her—ever so gently, of course—that though they had slept together, she should be careful to remember the agreement they had made?

After Andrea left, Shauna sat at her desk for a long time, staring at nothingness. Andrea was right; she had forgotten, in the magic of last night, that all they had promised each other was a year. A year, or as much time as it took to keep Mandy safe. And, while that might mean more than a year, it might also mean less...

Funny, she thought. Until Andrea had brought his name up, she had almost entirely forgotten Greg. She closed her eyes and tried to reconstruct her thoughts last night. Not once, she realised, had the memory of Greg entered her mind. Not once had she wished that it could be him beside her, instead of Rob...

I wonder, she asked herself bleakly, just how long ago it was that I fell in love with my husband?

She called the clinic and instructed Rob's nurse to tell him that something had come up and she couldn't take the afternoon off. She left it deliberately vague; she only knew that she couldn't face him just now. She spent the afternoon with her clients, but all the time she was studying balance sheets and financial statements and tax plans, her nerves were throbbing with the shock of knowledge.

Love—she had fallen in love with Rob. The unthinkable idea, once considered, refused to go away. Andrea's words had precipitated it, but the knowledge had been just under the surface of her conscious mind for some time, she thought. It was there as firmly as if it had been engraved in her bones, and she could not deny the truth of it. At some undefined moment in the past few weeks she had crossed the line from respect to love, from admiration of the way the man practised his profession to an aching desire to be a real part of his life, a permanent part, and to share with him all that two human beings could share. It was a heart-stopping realisation, almost more than Shauna could bear to face.

How could I have been so foolish? she asked herself. I wrote the terms myself, and now I'm caught in them.

She had been so careful to ensure, when she and Andrea had put together the pre-nuptial agreement, that there would be no entanglements at the end of this year together, nothing that would make it necessary for them to ever see each other again, or be reminded that once they had been husband and wife. She had been determined that once this episode was past, it would not be allowed to come back to haunt her.

She had used the power of her money to insulate herself, and now it had backfired on her. For it had never occurred to Shauna that, by the time it was over, she might not want him to leave.

Louise was in the kitchen, and the aroma of frying chicken was wafting through the flat. She looked up as Shauna came in. 'I thought this would be easier for you,' she said with a knowing smile. 'I'll just leave it in the oven.'

Shauna bit her tongue and went on into the big living-room, where Mandy was curled up with a book. The child turned a page and looked up. 'Rob said he'd be back in a little while.'

'Oh? Where did he go?'

'Out to play tennis with Amy Evans.'

The bitter bile of jealousy rose in Shauna's throat. It didn't take him long to console himself and find someone else to entertain him on his afternoon off, a little voice in the back of her brain pointed out. The sensation shocked her; my God, she thought, I've never felt this way before—not about Greg, not about anyone...

She said, holding her voice carefully level, 'Did he tell you that's who he was playing with?'

Mandy shook her head. Her eyes were fixed on the page again, and she sounded impatient. 'He didn't have to tell me. She was with him when he came home to change clothes.'

He had brought Amy Evans here? There was a throbbing anger deep inside Shauna; she fought it down with an effort. Don't be ridiculous, she told herself. It's his home now, too; he has every right to bring people in. And he knew Mandy would be here. He wouldn't have dared to bring Amy here if he had anything to hide.

'What do you think of her?' Shauna asked.

Mandy looked up over her glasses. 'She's just like you,' she said.

Shauna wanted to scream at the very idea.

'Always wanting to chat just when I get into a good part of my book. And to answer your next question— yes, I asked her to sit down, and I talked to her like a lady the whole time Rob was changing clothes. And it took him for ever, too. They'd been to lunch at Angelo's.'

He took her to lunch, too, Shauna thought. It was a bitter, stabbing hurt. He didn't invite me to lunch. Not that I would have gone, not today...

'Anything else you want to know?'

Shauna couldn't help but smile at the long-suffering tone. 'As a matter of fact, yes. Have you done your piano practice?' She saw a crafty look come into

Mandy's eyes, and reminded, 'I could ask Louise, you know.'

'You'd do it, too, wouldn't you?' Mandy put her book down with a sigh. 'I can't get away with anything around here. Mother always forgot to check.'

Shauna paused at the door. 'See? There were some advantages to living with her, after all.' But she wasn't thinking about Mandy's piano, or about Jessica. It was some comfort, she told herself, to know that at least Amy hadn't gone back to the bedroom wing with Rob while he changed clothes——

Clothes! No wonder Mandy had said it had taken him for ever. Louise had moved his clothes into Shauna's bedroom.

That's just great, Shauna, she told herself. How are you going to get out of this one?

Because there was no question of continuing down the road they had travelled last night, she knew. The mistakes she had already made could not be corrected, but she could certainly keep from making any more. To continue to sleep with Rob would be to court madness. She had to stop it now, while she still had her judgement, while she could still remember the terms of their agreement and protect herself from the consequences of forgetting.

Rob was teasing Mandy in the kitchen when she came back, after changing her pale yellow suit for shorts and a brief top. Louise was gone by then, and the two of them were exploring the contents of the oven.

He turned the moment she came in and watched as she walked across the room. 'Nice legs,' he murmured with a smile, and reached for her.

Shauna stepped aside and said, 'If you two will stop playing with the food and get washed up, we'll have dinner.' It came out a little more sharply than she had intended, and Mandy looked at her in surprise.

Rob looked stunned. Then he glanced at his watch. 'Sorry I'm late,' he said. 'It took longer for Amy to beat me than usual, and I haven't even had a shower.'

Shauna bit her lip. 'Don't bother,' she said. 'We'll just eat in the kitchen.'

'Good,' Mandy said. 'All this formal stuff wears me out.'

Shauna pushed her food around on her plate, trying to make it look as if she was eating. What she tried to chew tasted like wet cardboard. Her face felt hot, and she knew that Rob was watching her, with cautious concern in his face.

I have to talk about something, she thought. This silence is impossible. Finally, she said, too calmly, 'How was lunch?'

'Fine. I took Amy to Angelo's.' It was deliberate, as if he was determined she should know.

'I heard,' Shauna said sweetly.

'Is that what's bothering you? I had some things to talk to her about, and since you couldn't get away from the office, I thought today would be as good a time as any——'

'It was a busy day.' Her voice was light, almost flippant. 'And I certainly don't mind you taking Amy to lunch.'

He didn't look at her. 'Of course not. Why should you mind?'

The truth is, she admitted, I mind horribly. You've got only yourself to blame, Shauna, she thought. You could have spent the afternoon with him. You could have played tennis with him, you would probably have gone to bed with him—— Stop it, she told herself.

She pushed a bite of broccoli around on her plate. 'Are you thinking about going on with your studies, to specialise?'

'Why do you ask?'

Shauna shrugged. 'Well, you said you hadn't made up your mind about joining the practice. I just thought that might be what you wanted to talk to Amy about.'

'As a matter of fact, it was.'

He didn't sound very happy about it, though, she thought. Well, that makes two of us... 'Have patience, Rob. You'll be able to do anything you like——' She looked across at Mandy and bit off the rest of the sentence. *You'll be able to do anything you like in a year*, she wanted to say, but they had decided there was no need for Mandy to know about their agreement, and so she didn't say it. It hurt Shauna even to think the words, but she knew she had to. She must remind herself at every opportunity that this was only temporary. Then, perhaps, when their time together was up, it would not hurt so much.

It was obvious, she thought, that Rob knew what she had wanted to say, and his answer confirmed it. 'Who knows what another year will bring?' he said. 'No one is promised for ever, Shauna.' He cleared the plates away and put her uneaten food down the waste disposal. 'Is your homework done, Mandy?'

'There's a really good television show on——' Mandy began.

'Homework first,' Shauna said automatically.

Mandy looked from one of them to the other. 'Do you two have to agree on everything?' she asked tartly. 'It isn't fair to gang up on me, you know.'

After Mandy left the kitchen, Rob started to laugh. 'I have the impression that Mandy thought we were going to be pushovers,' he mused. He came across the room to her. 'What's bothering you, Shauna?' His voice was soft, almost caressing. 'It's apparent that you've had a hell of a day—you didn't eat, and you're so tense you look as if you're going to shatter. Speaking from experience,' he added huskily, 'I'd say a back rub and a sympathetic ear would do you a lot of good. If you'd like to try it——'

'No, thank you,' she said crisply. 'I think that's likely to lead to trouble.'

Rob's eyebrows went up. He perched on the corner of the table, his arms folded across his chest, and looked down at her. His feet were planted wide apart; one brown leg brushed against her knee. Shauna twisted her bare feet together under the table and stared at her place mat.

'As it did last night?' he said drily. 'Is sympathy all it was, then? You felt sorry for me last night, and that was your way of showing it?'

She didn't look at him. It hurt her soul to have what had happened between them last night reduced to a mere gesture of compassion; yet to tell him what it had really meant to her would lead to questions and explanations and embarrassing truths that would lie between them like a wall, impossible to surmount. To tell him that she loved him—in the first place, she thought, he probably wouldn't believe it. But if he did, he would feel sorry for her——

Shauna shivered. If there is one thing I cannot stand, she thought, it is that. I cannot bear for him to pity me.

What difference does it make what he thinks, she told herself, if I can only keep my folly to myself? If he never finds out how incredibly foolish I was, to fall in love with him——

'I suppose that's what it must have been,' she said, with a shrug.

His face had tightened into a mask. 'I see,' he said. 'And I suppose my clothes walked into your bedroom by themselves?'

She looked past him. 'Louise moved them. It's a problem with employees who have been around for years—they sometimes think they know best——' It wasn't quite a lie, she soothed her jittery conscience.

'Charming of her, wasn't it? Don't worry, Shauna, I don't have to have things written on billboards to get the message.' He slid off the table and disappeared down the hall.

Well, she thought, that's that. And I'm glad. Better to end it now than to live any longer in that fool's paradise I was in last night, and be hurt a thousand times worse in the end...

She noticed idly that her hands were shaking. She flipped through the mail that Louise had left lying on the kitchen desk; she didn't even see the return addresses. Mandy's pictures from the wedding were still lying on the counter, too, and she picked them up.

I'll have to get an album for them, she thought. It would please Mandy, and since they are the only record we have, I don't want to lose track of them.

She looked through the photographs. Funny, she thought, how different they looked today. She stared down at a picture of her and Rob, with his parents beside them. Shauna was holding the orchid bouquet.

I wonder, she thought, if I already loved him then. And what about Rob? What had he felt that day?

She couldn't see the expression in his eyes. The only thing that was perfectly in focus in the photograph was her bouquet.

Orchids, she thought. How did he know that I love them so? Did that mean anything at all? Surely he wouldn't have gone to so much trouble if I didn't matter a little...

Of course I matter, she reflected. I'm the fairy-tale godmother who will make it possible for him to go back to school as soon as Mother's not a threat any more. But as for me—the real me, not the McCoy money—I don't matter to him at all.

What an idiot I am, she thought. Because I know it all, and I would still like to go back to living in my fool's paradise, for however brief a time...

She started for her bedroom; he was just coming out of the little room at the end of the hall. He had showered and changed, and she could see past him to the clothes piled on the bed. He hadn't wasted any time in turning Louise's careful work upside-down. Well, who could blame him? she thought.

'I'm going out for a while,' he said shortly.

Something snapped deep inside Shauna, letting loose a flood of anger, laced with something that could only be stark terror. What if he doesn't come back? she thought. 'Shall I expect you home tonight?' she asked. Her voice was curt.

'Right now, I haven't any idea. Don't lie awake wondering what I'm doing if I don't come back, though—I won't be with another woman. A man isn't much success as a lover when his self-esteem has been destroyed, and you've been quite effective at that today, Shauna.'

'You should know,' she said sweetly. 'About what it takes to be a successful lover, I mean. It was rather obvious last night that I'm not the first woman in your life.'

'And you're not likely to be the last,' he said harshly. 'But don't let it worry you—as long as you're my wife, there won't be any other women, because I keep my promises, Shauna. Too bad we can't say the same for you.'

She heard the front door slam, and she sagged against the wall. Then she made her way into his little room and sank down beside his desk; it was the nearest chair, and right now she needed all the support she could find.

You're a fool, she told herself, an insanely jealous fool, so frightened of being hurt that you've been busily throwing away any chance you had to make things better.

For Rob was gone, and he might never come back at all, and suddenly she knew that anything would be better than this awful emptiness of loss. A week or a month or a year—what difference did it make if she could only have him for a brief time? Each day could be a precious memory—a treasure to hug close to her heart——

What was it Rob had said? 'No one is promised for ever,' that was it. There were no guarantees. Only today mattered. They might have a year full of days together...

'I can have a year of joy,' she whispered, 'or none at all.'

Rob is everything I've ever wanted, she thought. He's devoted to his job; he's a warm and gentle man, full of humour and kindness. He's a wonderful lover; he's the kind of person I want to be my friend as well as my husband, for however brief a time.

She looked up, and there above his desk, thumb-tacked to the wall, was a photograph. It was the picture Mandy had taken of Amy Evans, sitting beside Shauna in Andrea's living-room, less than an hour after Shauna had married the man Amy loved...

I felt so sorry for her, Shauna thought. My God, even then I knew, deep down somewhere, that I wanted him. And I was so certain I would win.

But the fact was, Rob had simply accepted the bargain she had driven, and now Shauna was the one who would have to pay, for the rest of her life...

I wonder, she thought, if Amy feels sorry for me, now. I wonder...

CHAPTER NINE

SHAUNA might have sat there for ever if the shrill ringing of the telephone hadn't startled her. Mandy answered it in the living-room and then came looking for her. 'It's Mother,' she said.

Shauna knew she shouldn't have been surprised; if the *hacienda* Rudy had leased didn't have a telephone, Jessica would have installed one by now if she'd had to run the wire herself.

But I got a letter from her just yesterday, Shauna thought. And why must she choose tonight, of all nights, to call? She's only been gone three weeks—what on earth could she want now?

The most likely thing, she decided, was that Jessica wanted a sympathetic ear for her complaints—the kind of luxurious wallowing in self-pity that simply wasn't available by mail. Shauna felt her stomach tightening at the very idea of having to listen cheerfully to her mother's woes, when all she wanted to do was slip off somewhere and have a good cry all by herself.

But Jessica surprised her. Her voice was clear, cheerful and calm, and she even enquired about Mandy's health and her state of mind, though she didn't seem to pay much attention to the answers. Then she said, 'Actually, Shauna, I'm calling to invite you and the doctor to a party I'm having next weekend. Do say you'll come. I'm having some wonderful people in——'

'Mother, I'm afraid it's impossible. We can't just fly to Mexico for a party. I'm sure we'd enjoy your friends, but——' Stretching the facts when talking to Jessica,

148

she had always thought, wasn't really the same as lying. And it was so much better than brittle truth...

Jessica laughed, the little escalating trill that announced she was about to say something witty. 'Oh, not in Mexico, Shauna. Didn't I tell you? I'm in St Louis. *Hacienda* living was just too awful, so I decided to come home.'

'You're in St Louis, Mother?' Shauna felt as if she'd been hit in the stomach with the telephone receiver. But of course, she told herself. I should have realised right away that this isn't a long-distance connection. It's too clear. But it never occurred to me that she might have come home——

Mandy looked up from her book. Her eyes were dilated in panic.

Jessica added briskly, 'We really must get together and discuss the astounding things that have been happening in my life, though I don't know when. I'm so busy at the moment. But we'll find time. Perhaps at the party——'

Shauna wet her lips. 'Did Rudy come home with you?' *Are you home to stay?*—that was what she really wanted to ask, but she didn't dare.

'No, he's still persisting with his silly movie. But he'll be here for the party. It's Friday night, at the house—I really insist that you come, Shauna. I have to hang up now; there are so many details to arrange.'

'I'll certainly talk to Rob about it and let you know.' She put the telephone down. Parties, she thought. Jessica had time to plan a party, but not to spend fifteen minutes discussing Mandy. She hadn't even said anything about wanting to see Mandy.

And just as well, too, Shauna told herself. The less interest Jessica showed in the child, the less likely it was that she would make an attempt to get her back. I could have faced this in a year, she thought, but not now. Oh, please, Mother, don't upset things right now——

Mandy was still looking frightened. 'Is she going to make me come back?' she whispered.

'No, darling. In any case, Rob and I would have a few things to say about that, if she even tried.' She gave the child a hug. 'You are going to stay right here.'

It seemed to satisfy Mandy. Shauna never quite knew how she managed to make it through the rest of the evening, but it was apparent that Mandy's suspicions had been successfully lulled.

When Shauna went in to kiss the child goodnight, she was already tucked in, with the lights turned out, her battered teddy bear held close, and Sol Abrams's recording of Beethoven's *Moonlight Sonata* playing softly on her stereo.

Mandy played her father's records less often these days, and when she did, she seemed to be happier about it. As if, Shauna thought, she no longer needed to escape into the music, and therefore she was free to enjoy it. That alone was worth the effort and the pain she herself had gone through, Shauna thought. At least, she could tell herself that, and hope that some day she could really believe it.

Mandy's voice caught her at the door, on her way out. 'Shauna,' she said, with a yawn, 'it's so lovely, isn't it— the way it's all worked out? And now that Mother's come back, isn't it lucky that I've got you and Rob, so I don't have to go and live with her again?'

Shauna swallowed hard. 'Yes, Mandy,' she heard herself say, in a low, throaty voice. 'It's lovely.'

Then she went to her own room and cried until her anger and hurt and frustration had drained away, leaving her body exhausted and numb. Only then, as she lay across her bed, her face buried in a pillow, could she begin to think clearly again.

There was still no sign of Rob. Despite what he had said about not seeking out another woman, she thought she could probably find him easily enough, by calling

Amy's apartment. But that wouldn't help anything; it would probably only make him angrier.

But she had to find a way to patch everything back together, and make it possible for the two of them to play the happily married couple again, for Jessica's benefit . . .

This morning, she thought painfully, we didn't have to pretend. For a few hours, we really were a happily married couple. And it wasn't just the fact that we had spent the night in the same bed, either. It was much more than making love that brought us together—it was sharing Rob's pain over his little patient, and the nurturing comfort we found in each other's arms. And I, like an idiot, ruined it all with my jealous rage. I wanted more, and so, in my confusion, I tossed out the wonderful things I already had——

She put her hands to her temples, trying to still the throbbing there, the echoing refrain that kept whispering, 'It's too late.' Because it couldn't be too late. For Mandy's sake, she couldn't let it be too late——

Rob must have felt those things too, she thought, and a trace of hope flickered through her veins. He had needed her last night—needed her strength and her courage and her faith—as surely as she needed him now. Today, of course, she had undermined all of that, as efficiently as if she had used dynamite. But wait, a little voice argued. Wasn't that, in its own way, a positive sign? If he was completely indifferent to her, then how could it have been possible for her to wound his pride, his self-esteem?

She thought it over, and rejected the idea as wishful thinking. 'In any case,' she muttered, 'it hardly matters now.' What if he didn't come back at all? She would still have to warn him about Jessica.

She found Amy's telephone number tacked up on the wall above Rob's desk, as if he used it often. When the telephone started to ring, she nearly broke the connection; what could she say, after all? 'Send my husband home, immediately'?

When a low feminine voice answered, Shauna gulped. 'This is Shauna McCoy,' she began hoarsely, and then corrected herself. 'Shauna Stevens. Is my husband there?'

There was a pause, and a rustle. Shauna gripped the receiver and closed her eyes in pain. She could almost see Amy making frantic signals to Rob——

'No, he's not,' the low voice said.

I don't believe you for a moment, Shauna wanted to scream. She swallowed hard, trying to think what she should do next. 'Would you tell him I have to talk to him?'

'I don't expect to see him. He was here, but he left some time ago. You're a fool, you know.'

'How kind of you to tell me that,' Shauna snapped. 'Though what makes you think it's any of your business——'

'It's my business when I see a brilliant young doctor tied down and unable to do his best work.'

'Rob knows quite well that his future is entirely up to him,' Shauna said. She was astounded that she could sound so calm.

'Not as long as you're holding him back.' It was cold.

'It is not my intention to hold him back for ever, Dr Evans.'

'Good,' Amy Evans said, and hung up.

Shauna felt a little sick as she put the telephone down. I wish I could let him go right now, she thought. It would be better for us both. But I can't. Not till I know that Mandy is safe. Then I'll let him go——

Don't fool yourself into thinking you're being generous, her conscience reminded her. You can't take credit for unselfishness when you give up something that you never really had.

Did he love Amy? The young woman certainly cared for him, and they had so much in common that it could hardly be a surprise if they wanted to spend their lives together. It made her whole body hurt just to think about it.

She went to wash the salt tears off her face. He had to come back some time, she told herself. She had an apology to make, and she intended to be waiting, whenever he came home.

She left the lamps off and sat in the corner of the living-room, looking like a ghost in her white satin robe. Down on the river the bright lights still glowed on the showboats lined up along the levee, and gleamed off the shimmery skin of the Gateway Arch. It seemed as if she sat there for a long time, waiting, and thinking of nothing, because she did not dare to think.

When his key clicked in the lock, she thought for an instant that her heart would never beat again. Then the door swung wide, and she stood up to face him.

The dim moonlight did not penetrate to the door, and in his dark clothes he was barely a silhouette. Shauna knew that her face would be no more than a pale oval, her satin robe a blur. Perhaps it would be easier, she thought, to say what she had to say in the dark.

'Rob,' she said, very softly, 'I am most horribly sorry for the things I said tonight.' Her voice shook. She clenched her hands together; her palms were wet.

He seemed to freeze, and then he turned towards her as if there was nothing in the world he wanted less to see.

'I was afraid you wouldn't come back,' she whispered.

'I almost didn't,' he said ruefully. 'I half expected you would have told the doorman to call the police if I showed up here again.'

She shook her head wearily. 'No, not that.' I have to get it all clear, she thought. 'Rob, I talked to Amy tonight. She seems to think I'm sabotaging your career on purpose.'

'Shauna, I can explain——'

'Please. You don't owe me an explanation, and I have no desire to hear one.' It was quiet, but it was firm. 'I told her—and I want you to know—that I certainly don't intend to interfere in your life a moment longer than I have to.'

She felt a sudden, desperate need to put it all into words, to convince herself as well as him. 'You've promised me a year,' she said softly, 'or whatever it takes to keep Mandy safely out of Mother's hands. What you do after that will not be my concern. What I do will be none of your business. It simply won't matter.' She thought for a moment that the lie would choke her, but what else was there for her to say?

She had to force herself to speak again. 'This marriage has been more difficult than either of us thought it could possibly be——'

He said something under his breath. She thought it was, 'That's the truth,' but she wasn't sure.

She went on, steadying her voice with an effort. 'I would release you from your promise now if I could, Rob, but there's still Mandy. I can't take any chances with Mandy right now, because——' She gulped, and said, very softly, 'My mother is back in town.'

'Oh, God.' It sounded as if the words were wrung from him.

She tensed and said quickly, 'That's not why I'm apologising. I was dead wrong today, and that has nothing to do with Mother. But I'm begging you, Rob. Please, can we just forget about today, and start over again—for Mandy's sake? Make the best of it, for as long as we have to?'

There was a long silence, and then he moved into the light, towards her. 'It seems that we spend a lot of time starting over.' She realised that he was holding something, and her nose caught the spicy scent of carnations. 'Do you know how hard it is to buy flowers at this time of night?' he mused.

Flowers. Not only had he come back, but he had brought her flowers... She gulped and wiped a stray tear off her cheek and shook her head.

He put the carnations into her hands. 'We've both said a lot of things tonight that would be better forgotten, Shauna. I'm sorry, too——'

She nodded miserably. 'We have a year, Rob. We can still make it a pleasant time——'

He didn't move. There seemed to be nothing else to say. She held the carnations to her nose and breathed their spicy scent, and then she said, 'I'm going to bed, Rob. Come in, if—if you like.' It was no more than a whisper, and she fled down the hall to hide the tears that threatened.

If only I had been wise enough today not to ask senseless questions about the future, she thought. Then I could have gone to sleep tonight happy merely because he was beside me...

He came in while she was brushing her hair, and took the brush from her hand. Neither of them spoke for a long time; the rhythmic strokes made her hair fall in a gleaming river almost to her waist. When he was finished, he set the brush back on the dressing-table, and stooped to kiss her, just as he used to do, and she knew he was going to go away, to the little room at the end of the hallway. She caught his hand. 'Please, Rob,' she said. 'Don't leave me.'

He looked surprised, and she bit her lip and tried to fight down the colour that fluttered in her cheeks. 'You needn't make love to me,' she whispered. 'Just hold me——'

He sighed. 'All right,' he said. 'If that's what you want, Shauna.'

She was restless, and every time she moved in his arms, she could feel the tension course through his body. He hates being here, she thought. I should have let him go.

'Would you just go to sleep?' he hissed finally.

'I'm not sleepy. I'm sorry——' She turned against him. He shifted slightly and for a moment her body pressed close against his. It was accidental, but the contact brought hot colour to her face and relief to her heart, for his body could not lie about what he wanted. She let her hand slip down his chest and across his flat stomach, her touch fleeting and gentle.

He caught her fingers. 'Shauna,' he warned, 'if you don't want trouble, you'd better stop now. I am only human, you know, and I should never have let you talk me into lying in this bed and trying to forget that you're here beside me, half-naked and so damned beautiful that——'

Desire is a trap either of us could be caught in...

'I said we didn't have to make love, Rob,' she reminded quietly. 'But if we want to, that's something else again——'

He groaned and pulled her close. His lovemaking was not gentle, but she exulted in it; the wildness of the storm that caught them up fulfilled a hunger deep inside her. He needed her, and he wanted her, and for the moment that was all the satisfaction she could ask for.

It certainly isn't everything I want, she thought, but for now, it is enough. I do not dare allow myself to want more.

This, Shauna told herself in the days that followed, was the darker side of loving. Their days were filled with carefully casual politeness, but in the stillness of the nights, after he went to sleep, sometimes her pillow blotted silent tears. And each time he made love to her, she feared that this might be the last.

Her love for him seemed to catch her by the throat each time he walked into the room, and sometimes she had to turn away to get control of herself, before she could look up at him and smile, and pretend that everything was just fine in her little world, and that her heart wasn't aching with fear of what she knew lay somewhere in her future, just barely out of sight.

Jessica's party was set for Friday evening, and that morning at the breakfast table Rob promised faithfully that he would be out of the clinic with plenty of time to spare.

Shauna, who had heard that promise before, and who knew exactly what it was worth, said, 'All the same, I think I'll call Andrea. I hate to make my entrance alone, especially to one of Mother's parties, and if you're late——'

'Shauna, I'll be here. Have I ever forgotten something this important?'

She nodded. 'Frequently. There is the matter of your electricity bills, for instance——'

He scowled at her over his coffee-cup. 'That was a long time ago. I haven't done anything of the sort recently.'

'Only because I've got your cheque book now.' She giggled. 'Oh, don't take it personally, for heaven's sake. I don't.' It was odd, but true, she thought. Once, she had wondered what kind of a woman would put up with a man who couldn't even remember to pay his bills. Now she knew. I would put up with it for ever, without so much as a whimper, she thought. To have Rob, I'd put up with a whole lot more than that, because there are so many other things about him that I love...

She walked around the table to stand behind him, and leaned over to kiss his cheek. He looked up as if he was surprised at the gesture, and she broke it off. She was a bit frightened of the flood of tenderness that such a simple caress could release within her.

His fingers crept to the back of her neck and held her while his mouth brushed hers. It was a simple caress, and yet she began to feel just a little dizzy.

It was foolish, she told herself, to go all soft and silly over a kiss, when she was sleeping with the man every night. This morning he had awakened her at dawn, and made love to her so tenderly that her heart still ached with longing...

Remember, Shauna, she warned herself. Remember that the future doesn't come with a guarantee.

She sighed, and he quickly let her go, and she felt almost abandoned.

'I'll be home,' he said. 'I wouldn't think of leaving you to face your mother's party alone.'

But he did. She hadn't called Andrea after all, so she paced the parquet floor in the entrance hall and waited for Rob. Louise had long since gone home, and Mandy was spending the weekend with a schoolfriend, so the flat was silent.

Rob didn't come, and he didn't call, and though Shauna knew that there must be a sensible explanation, it made her furious anyway. When she finally telephoned the clinic and got only the answering service, she was ready to explode. 'He could at least have called!' she stormed, and went down to her Jaguar.

The party had been going on for a full hour by the time she arrived. She turned her car over to the valet at the door, and tried to shake the wrinkles from her temper, as well as from the skirt of her moss-green cocktail dress, before she climbed the steps. She hadn't even seen her mother yet, and Shauna wasn't about to let Jessica suspect that all might not be well in the Stevens's household. 'I'll just wait till Rob appears,' she muttered to herself, 'and then I'll take him apart in private for standing me up!'

Irritation carried her through the worst of it. She greeted her mother with a kiss on the cheek and was introduced to the famous actor who was standing beside Jessica. Joshua Reynolds had been a fixture on the American screen for years. Shauna glanced around and realised that there were plenty of other famous faces, too.

So that's the reason for the party, Shauna thought. Mother is showing off her new toys. I feel as though I ought to curtsy, or something——

She restrained herself with an effort, and made polite conversation for a few moments. Josh Reynolds unbent to a surprising degree, asking her about St Louis and about her job. He's a little bit like Sol, she thought; the memory of the man who had been her favourite step-father made her ache just a little. If only Sol hadn't died, things would be so different. For Mandy, for me, perhaps even for Jessica...

Rudy was at the bar, leaning on the rail, when Shauna strolled over. 'I didn't know Josh Reynolds was going to be in your movie, Rudy.'

He turned slowly towards her. 'He's not. I've changed my mind.' His eyes slid over her shoulder to focus on Jessica.

It doesn't mean anything, Rudy, she wanted to say. For as long as Shauna could remember, there had never been a party where the best-looking man in the room wasn't glued to Jessica's side. Next week, or next month, the face would be different, but the view would be the same.

Rudy looked back at her. 'Can I get you a drink, Shauna?'

'Please. Do you have a new speciality by now?'

He nodded. 'I call it Mexican Madness.'

'That sounds dangerous enough to be attractive.'

He gestured to the bartender, and then sipped from his own glass. 'Where's your young man tonight?'

'He'll be along later.' She tasted the drink, warily. 'Rob often works very late—too many patients, you know.' She kept her tone light, casual.

A smooth voice beside her said, 'I didn't think it was possible for anyone to have more of a devotion to duty than you do, Shauna.'

'Hello, Greg.' Of course, she told herself, she should have known Greg would be here—he was still one of Jessica's favourite men—but she hadn't even given it a thought. That would no doubt surprise him, she concluded.

'He must be very tiresome, this doctor of yours, to say nothing of stupid, to leave you here alone. Or doesn't he appreciate how very beautiful you are?'

'Oh, he appreciates me.' It was almost funny, she thought, to remember how Greg's low, suggestive murmur used to send sexy chills up her spine. The truth was that she hadn't really known what sexy meant till she met Rob.

She smiled to herself, remembering the night Rob had come to her apartment to talk about Mandy, and ended by shaking her hand at the door. And I actually believed he didn't know anything about how to treat a woman, she thought.

'Is there something amusing about me?' Greg looked down at her over the rim of his Scotch glass.

'Personal joke. Too silly to share.' She didn't bother to repress the smile.

'Perhaps we should go off somewhere and talk about old times,' he suggested with a sultry softness in his voice.

'Later,' Shauna said drily.

'As you wish.' He raised his glass to her, and slipped off into the crowd.

'Much later,' she muttered. 'And only if I don't see you coming.'

'Talking to yourself?' Andrea slipped through the crowd to her side. 'It's a sign of old age, I understand. I was beginning to think you had decided to sit the party out.'

'I nearly did, and Rob certainly has.'

Andrea looked her over thoughtfully, through half-closed eyes. 'Mad at him?'

'Well, he did say he'd be here. I don't blame him, exactly, because as parties go this is deadly boring, and I'm sure that whatever Rob is doing is more exciting than watching Mother flirt with Josh Reynolds, but still——'

'Don't vent your anger on Rob just because your mother looks younger than you do tonight.'

Shauna turned to study Jessica with narrowed eyes. She hadn't thought of it, but Andrea was right. Jessica was wearing a floating black creation that had no back and not much of a front, and in the candlelight she looked about twenty-four.

'Isn't it wonderful,' Andrea murmured, 'what an absence of responsibility can do for a woman's looks? She's got ten years younger since you took Mandy off her hands. Of course, as you say, having Josh Reynolds around couldn't hurt. Is Rob coming later?'

'Your guess is as good as mine. For all I know, he thinks the party is next week.' She turned back to the bartender for another drink. It might be foolish, because one never quite knew what was in Rudy's special concoctions, but she didn't care.

Andrea gave her a speculative look. 'Shauna, be careful. You look a bit reckless tonight.'

'Is that a warning or a compliment?' Shauna didn't wait for an answer. She drifted off towards the front hallway, where Josh Reynolds was doing his version of a flamenco on the marble floor, with the crowd cheering him on.

Jessica beckoned her over. 'Poor darling,' she cooed. 'How do you stand it when your brand-new husband leaves you alone like this?'

The solicitude made Shauna bristle, but it also fed the flame of her irritation with Rob. He could have called and told me what was holding him up, she thought. The way it is, if I make excuses for him, and then he comes in with a different explanation, we'll both look like colossal liars. And if I say I haven't any idea what he's doing—well, that certainly ought to amuse Mother!

'Rob has a very busy practice,' she said coldly.

'Of course. I suppose I really shouldn't say things like that about him. All the same, I wouldn't put up with it myself.'

And she wouldn't, Shauna thought. But there was no sense in discussing it.

'There's Greg, darling.' Jessica beckoned to him across the room. 'He's here alone tonight, too. He's heart-broken, you know. He expected you to come to your senses before this, and when you married that—young man—on the rebound...'

'It had nothing to do with Greg, Mother.' Shauna realised, a little too late, that the last thing she wanted to do was prompt Jessica to wonder just why she had married Rob. So she smiled up at Greg and said, 'Let's go and dance. I think you said you wanted to talk about old times?' I would do anything, she told herself, to get away from Jessica just now.

The band began a slow number, and Greg pulled her so close that Shauna was glad Rob wasn't there to see. I used to dance with him like this, she thought. But it's changed, now. There is only one man I want to be this close to, now——

But keeping at a safe distance was like pulling herself out of quicksand; every time she won an inch, Greg pulled her back against him. Without stamping on his toes or making a public struggle of it, there was not much she could do, but when he said, 'I really do want to talk to you,' Shauna nodded. Anything, she thought, would be better than this.

She didn't resist when he pulled her out of the hallway and into a little sitting-room. If he was going to plead with her, she thought, she'd much rather have it be private.

But he didn't seem to know how to begin. He took her hand. Finally he said, 'You gave me a lot to think about, you know, when you broke our engagement.'

'I certainly hope so.'

'For a long time, I thought you were being terribly rigid and foolish. Now—well, now I see it differently. I'm going to get my son back, Shauna.'

She could scarcely believe what she was hearing. For a single instant, she could see the round face, the big brown eyes, the charming smile, of Greg's baby son, as she had seen them the day the child's mother had come to tell her the truth. Shauna had not wanted to admit that any man could turn his back on a child, and especially not a child as beautiful as that one. But now Greg had finally realised where his responsibility lay, and what he was missing in not knowing his son. It helped to heal the hurt that she had felt, when she realised that she had actually cared for someone who was capable of such selfishness——

There were tears in her eyes as she turned to him, and her fingers clutched at his. 'I'm so glad, Greg,' she whispered. 'So very, very glad!'

His arms went around her, and suddenly he was kissing her with a passionate hunger that both startled and repelled her. 'I thought you'd see it that way,' he said, against her lips. 'It will be all right, then——'

'Greg, I don't understand——'

'You can get rid of this adventurer you've married, now, and we'll raise my boy together. I know how crazy you are about kids. We'll have some of our own, too, of course—as many as you want. I couldn't forget about you, Shauna. And if I have to take the kid to get you back, well, then——'

'Greg!' She tried to push him away, futilely.

His tongue probed her mouth, fiercely demanding. His hands were in her hair, seeking out the key pins that held the auburn waves up.

Shauna couldn't escape, she couldn't scream, she couldn't even lash out at him. My God, she thought, he's going to rape me right here and call it an act of love——

The sitting-room door opened. 'Get out,' Greg said. 'Private party.'

With the last of her strength, Shauna pushed him away. She turned towards the door to plead for help from this chance intruder——

Rob looked at her with the eyes of a stranger, and said, 'Your mother wants you, Shauna. Shall I tell her you'll be too busy to see her for a while?'

CHAPTER TEN

SHAUNA blinked, trying to make him disappear. She could cope with Greg alone, if she had to, she thought frantically. But Rob, standing there in the doorway, impossibly tall, impossibly handsome—and stunningly, blindingly angry—no, there would be no easy way to deal with him.

'You don't understand, Rob,' she whispered. She struggled to her feet, and stood there twisting her hands like a guilty child. Her hair had tumbled around her shoulders.

He shrugged. 'What's to understand? I thought it was obvious.'

For an instant, she thought she had imagined that, too, for he was calm, as if it didn't matter, as if he wasn't longing to rip her apart with his bare hands in fury——

'Are you coming with me?' he asked. 'Or would you prefer your privacy?'

Slowly, as she stood there, she realised that his anger existed only in her mind. He wasn't furious with her; there was simply no reaction at all, beyond a cool politeness that made her want to fly across the room at him and beat her fists against his handsome face until he showed some kind of emotion.

Damn you, Rob Stevens! she was screaming inside. Can't you at least pretend that I mean something to you?

That was what really hurt, she realised. Any normal husband, when confronted with the sight of his wife in the arms of another man, would demand an explanation from the wife, the other man, or both. But Rob simply didn't care, and the knowledge was like the edge of a razor slicing her heart into strips.

'I'll come with you,' she said.

'Shauna!' Greg protested. 'I won't let you walk away from what we've shared!'

She looked at him with loathing. My God, she thought, if he had acted just a little earlier, and taken responsibility for his baby son a few months ago, I would have married him. It wasn't the existence of the child that I couldn't forgive, it was the way Greg had treated him. If he had taken custody of that child, I would have pardoned the rest, without ever questioning his reasons— and what a tragedy that would have been, for all of us.

She wanted to spit on her mother's priceless Aubusson carpet, just to get rid of the taste of Greg—the man she had once thought she loved.

'You'd better straighten up your hair.' Rob leaned against the door, tapping his fingers impatiently on the casing, while she did her best to smooth the auburn waves back into some kind of order, and then held the door for her.

'Rob,' she said breathlessly. 'I can explain——'

'You don't owe me an explanation. And I have no desire to listen to one.' It was an echo of what she had told him the night of their quarrel; if he had sounded sarcastic or vengeful she would have felt comforted a bit. But his voice was expressionless, as if he really didn't remember that she had said those words to him first.

There was no one in the drawing-room; it looked as if it had been set up for a party of ghosts. Shauna stumbled on the loose edge of a rug, and Rob caught her. His hand was impersonal under her arm. He set her back on her feet and released her, as he would a stranger that he had helped to cross a street.

Her hand clenched tight on Rob's arm. Jessica was leaning against the grand piano in the front hallway, her black dress stark against the glossy white finish of the instrument. She was sipping from a champagne glass, and laughing up at Josh Reynolds, beside her. Then she turned and looked straight at Shauna, and beckoned her across the room. For the first time, Shauna began to wonder why she had been summoned.

What has Mother done now? Shauna asked herself. She's the one who sent Rob to look for me. Was she hoping that he'd find me as he did? Or did she go even farther than that, and set me up? Could she and Greg have planned it between them, making sure that Rob found me in an embarrassing position? Is she going to demand that I give Mandy back to her because my conduct proves I'm not a fit custodian for a child? She's capable of doing it, no matter how large the crowd. She never did care how much family laundry she aired in public——

She forced herself to smile. 'You wanted me, Mother?'

'Shauna, you look as if you've been mugged,' Jessica said flatly.

'Sorry,' Rob murmured. 'That's my fault. You know how newlyweds are when they haven't seen each other all day.' He smoothed a stray lock of Shauna's hair back into place.

She wanted to sag against him in thankful relief. Then she realised that it wasn't her he was trying to protect, but Mandy. It made her furious all over again.

Jessica looked him up and down, her expression making it apparent that she didn't believe a word of it. Then she turned to the crowd. 'For heaven's sake, have a good time. Rudy and I have just announced that we're separating, that's all. This is a celebration of our new lives, not a funeral.' She gestured to the leader of the band, who promptly struck up a fast number. A few people started to dance. She watched them for a moment and then turned to Shauna. 'Wish me happy, my dear.'

'New lives?' Shauna said grimly. 'Do you mean that you're getting a divorce?'

Jessica's eyes narrowed. 'Yes, I am, Shauna.'

'But——' Shauna looked up at the tall, handsome man hovering protectively beside her mother. 'Mother, I think you have gone completely berserk.' Her words were low and evenly spaced and expressionless. She turned to the actor. 'Mr Reynolds, you must realise what a foolish thing the two of you are doing——'

Rob's fingers bit into her arm. She tried to shake him off.

Jessica's eyes were cold. 'Josh, I beg your pardon for my daughter's lack of manners.'

The actor smiled at Shauna. 'I know you're shocked,' he said with easy charm. 'I thought Jessica should tell you earlier——'

'I wish that she hadn't bothered to tell me at all.'

'I think we should go home, darling,' Rob said. 'I'm not sure what Shauna's been drinking, Jessica, but she's obviously not at her best——'

'Thanks a million,' Shauna muttered as they stood on the doorstep, waiting for the valet to bring her Jaguar around. 'The crowning touch was for you to reply that I was too drunk to behave myself——'

For a moment it seemed that he wasn't even going to answer. Finally, he said, 'You certainly acted it. Besides, it was the only way I could think of to get you out of there before you really messed things up. Why on earth are you taking it personally, Shauna?'

She ignored the question. 'You're a fine one to talk about messing things up! You're hours late, and you didn't even bother to call. Where in the hell have you been, Rob Stevens?'

'At the hospital, with a newborn whose lungs weren't functioning right.'

'All this time?'

'Not quite, no. If you want the details,' he added crisply, 'Amy and I took five minutes for a cup of coffee in the doctors' lounge after we had the baby stabilised.'

I might have known, she thought, that it would be Amy. Amy Evans and a newborn infant—for Rob, it would always be one or the other...

'You could have called,' she said icily, 'instead of leaving me alone to face my mother's crazy idea of an engagement party!'

'I can't believe that you were surprised. I thought it was perfectly clear, the moment I walked in, what was going on. And she's certainly done it frequently enough.'

'Always before, she's got rid of one husband *before* she announced his successor,' Shauna said tartly. 'I realise that sounds like a minor point of etiquette, but it was rather an important one, I thought.'

'Oh?' He sounded mildly interested. 'I suppose that's why you were kissing your friend in the sitting-room instead of on the dance-floor——'

'That was my former fiancé,' she announced, with all the dignity she could muster. 'And he had just told me that he's going to be getting custody of his little son. Naturally, I was pleased for him——'

'Naturally,' Rob murmured. There was an ironic twist to his words.

She seized her car keys from the valet's hand. I would like to scratch my initials on my husband's face with them, she thought. 'Thank you for your concern, Rob, but I'll drive myself home. And don't worry, I am quite sober. I am furious with my mother, that's all——'

'I should think you'd be delighted.'

Shauna slid into the driver's seat and then popped back out to face him. 'What on earth do you mean? Why would I be delighted because she's making a first-class fool of herself?'

'Stop and think. She's not going to want Mandy sharing her new honeymoon cottage, that's for sure. And even if she did, as long as she's making an idiot of herself over Josh Reynolds, she would be laughed out of a court of law if she tried to sue you.'

'Oh.' Shauna folded herself back into the Jaguar's seat and stared thoughtfully through the windscreen. 'But she could still make things miserable if she tried,' she pointed out.

'She isn't going to. That was what she was going to tell you, if you hadn't made a scene. She'd already told me how grateful she was to you for taking Mandy off her hands like that. You should be proud, Shauna. You've single-handedly made it possible for Jessica to take up a wonderful new life in Hollywood.'

'If you think I'm going to take the blame for my mother's choices, Rob——'

He shrugged. 'Blame, credit—what difference does it make? The only thing that matters is that you don't need me any more at all.'

But I do, she thought blankly. I need you more than I ever did. Rob, can't you see?

'We are free. I suppose it would be prudent to wait a month or so before we actually split,' he added briskly. 'Just to let Jessica get settled. But there's no sense in dragging it out any longer than that, is there?'

She swallowed hard. Must he sound so fearsomely cheerful about it, when her heart was ripping itself quietly into bits? But of course, she thought, he must feel like a prisoner who has just received an unexpectedly early parole. Early enough that he could still follow Amy to the West Coast, if that was what he wanted...

'Whatever you think would be best,' she said. She put the Jaguar into gear and started home. She drove very carefully, because the tears in her eyes gave her double vision, and she knew if they once started to spill over, she would not be able to see at all.

You should be glad, she told herself. This never was a marriage; it was an endurance contest. It was doomed from the beginning, and you might as well admit it and be glad that you've got a chance to start over. You've got Mandy, and that's all you really wanted . . .

You're a liar, she told herself. And not a very good one—you can't even convince yourself.

She locked her bedroom door that night. The childish gesture made her feel better, until she realised that Rob neither knew nor cared that she had deliberately shut him out.

'So he's moving out,' Andrea said.

Shauna stared down into her coffee-cup and nodded. 'As soon as he finds an apartment—probably next week some time.' She didn't want to look at Andrea. She knew without checking that Andrea was wearing the same sort of face as when she was cross-examining a hostile witness. Shauna had been trying to avoid Andrea for three weeks, since the night of the party, but today the woman had arrived at her office without warning and announced that she was staying until she got answers. Shauna, who knew that stubborn look, had given up and told Andrea everything.

She had been a little surprised herself when Rob had said he was looking for an apartment; she had half expected that he would just move into Amy's for the next few weeks. But she supposed that nothing he did was any of her business now, and so she had withdrawn into silence instead of asking what his plans included.

He seemed to feel the same way. He was cheerful enough when Mandy was around, and he took her to the park, to the zoo. But after she went to bed, he retreated to the little room at the end of the hall, and he didn't come out again for anything . . .

Her bed felt big and empty and cold without him, and she lay there trying not to think of the last time he had made love to her . . .

She dragged herself back from dangerous ground.

'Well, I knew something was seriously wrong,' Andrea mused. 'You haven't looked like yourself since that stupid party, but I thought you were just disgusted with Jessica's behaviour. Why your mother insists on turning her life into a social strip-tease——'

'At least she's gone,' Shauna said. 'She'll fit right into Los Angeles. There, no one will even notice her eccentricities.' She walked across the room and stared out of the window. The same old view, she thought. Perhaps I should think about making a change—sell my share of the firm and do something else——

The truth was, she admitted painfully, that if Rob gave the least indication of wanting her, she would give her business away and follow him . . . That, she thought sardonically, would really give Andrea reason to doubt my sanity!

'Has she filed for divorce?'

'Yes. I got a note from her yesterday—she's already figured out which day it will be final. I'm sure as soon it is, she and Josh will be on the cover of the celebrity magazines——'

'They already have been,' Andrea said drily. 'Along with Rudy and his new love——' She paused at the startled look on Shauna's face. 'Didn't you know? That's why he fired Josh Reynolds—Rudy's rewriting the whole picture to star his future bride. Now that's a divorce that was really a mutual decision.'

Shauna groaned. 'And to think I was feeling sorry for him!'

Andrea refilled her cup from the pot on the corner of Shauna's desk. 'As long as we're talking about divorce, shall I start the paperwork on yours?'

Shauna nodded. It felt like she was tearing off her arm and giving it away. 'You might as well. But keep it quiet, Andrea. We haven't even told Mandy yet, because we thought there was no sense in upsetting her about it till Rob found a place to live.'

'Don't you think you should prepare her for the shock? It's going to be one, you know—she thinks Rob is the most perfect man on earth.'

'I know. All right, I'll tell you the truth—I know how miserable it's going to be living with Mandy when she finds out Rob's leaving, and I just can't take it any earlier than necessary.' She looked up sheepishly.

'She's got to suspect that something's wrong.'

'I don't know. We're being very polite to each other.'

'That's enough, right there. Mandy's not a fool.'

'You can say that again.' Shauna sighed. She had been trying for three weeks to figure out a way to tell Mandy, and the only thing she was certain of was that it was going to be nasty. 'I expect we'll have a whole new round of stomach-aches—in fact, I'm having some of my own already. I suppose it's only psychological; I must be trying to prepare myself to deal with Mandy's.'

'Bad ones?' Andrea asked idly.

'Bad enough that I even worked up my courage and asked Rob about the pain.'

'Good idea.'

'Some help he was. He told me to talk to a doctor. I said I thought that was what I was doing——'

Andrea smothered a smile. 'Well, it isn't precisely his speciality.'

'A stomach-ache is a stomach-ache.'

Andrea hadn't paused. 'You might ask him to give you the name of a good obstetrician, though. I'm sure he has a favourite.'

'I have a perfectly good doctor——' Shauna stopped dead. For a long instant she stared across the desk at her friend, and then she said with a sort of croak, 'Are you suggesting this might be morning sickness? But I couldn't possibly be pregnant!'

'Why couldn't you?' Andrea asked with mild interest. 'Unless you and Rob spent all your evenings playing tiddlywinks instead of indulging in more adult forms of entertainment, I should think it's quite possible.'

'Andrea, don't be foolish——'

'The pill has been known to fail.'

Shauna grabbed her calendar and started to do some hasty figuring. She wasn't altogether sure she'd been taking the pill—her mornings were blurred with misery. 'Four weeks,' she said. 'That's all it could be——' She looked up in horror. 'My God, Andrea, it is possible! You don't really think——'

Andrea shrugged. 'I'm no expert, but it seems logical. In any case, I wouldn't waste any time in finding out. If there's a baby on the way, you've got a lot of planning to do, and I'm not talking about knitting booties.'

Shauna shivered. 'That's not funny, Andrea.'

'I know it's not. Have you forgotten your pre-nuptial agreement? If you're pregnant, you've already agreed to give Rob the baby.'

Until that instant, Shauna had forgotten. 'You said that wouldn't stand up in court,' she reminded tersely.

'I don't think it will. But I'd really rather not test it out.'

Shauna sagged in her chair. My God, she thought. I thought it was a nightmare before, but this——

'Sue me for malpractice if you like,' Andrea said. 'I probably deserve it, for letting you agree to that clause. But see a doctor first, all right?'

She didn't ask Rob for the name of an obstetrician; she went to her regular doctor instead. She would find out first if she was pregnant, she had decided, and then she would figure out what to do about it. For she absolutely would not give up her child, no matter what sort of terms she had agreed to when she signed that stupid pre-nuptial agreement. He could fight her in court for the next eighteen years if he wanted, but she would not yield, not even if she had to take her baby and flee...

Away from the man I love, her heart cried. I've had to give him up already; surely it's too cruel to make me give up our child, too. Would Rob understand that? Or would he hold her to her promise, and take the baby?

Or was it just barely possible that a baby might change things altogether? If she stood firm about refusing to give the baby up, and if Rob would not consider being separated from his child—was there any possibility at all that they might find their way to a compromise? Perhaps his further training wasn't as important to him as his own child would be. And after all, he had married her—but only for the money, a little voice at the back of her brain reminded her.

The cycle of hope and despair repeated itself over and over, as she waited in the doctor's office for the verdict.

How long, she wondered miserably, could it possibly take to get the results of a pregnancy test? It seemed to be for ever. The doctor had recognised the desperation in her face, and had said, very gently, that he would call her with the results just as soon as he could, but Shauna had merely looked through him and said, 'I'll wait.'

She shifted impatiently in her chair in the corner of the examining room. Her hands were aching from the way they were clasped together. The yellow diamond cut into her palm, and she stared down at it. How innocent she had been that day, she thought, and how certain that she could control her life——

The door of the examining-room opened. The doctor came in, pulled his chair around, looked her straight in the eyes. 'The test is negative,' he said bluntly.

She looked at him for one stricken moment, and then she stared down at her fingers, twisted together in her lap. Only the pain seemed to be real just now. 'I'm not pregnant?' she whispered.

He shook his head. 'If these symptoms persist, we'll look a little farther for causes. But with the stressful few weeks you've described, it's really no wonder that you're having problems. Newlyweds' nerves—nothing to be concerned about, really.'

'Thank you,' she whispered, dutifully.

'There, now,' he said with a fatherly smile. 'I'm sure it's a relief to know that there won't be a baby just yet——'

'Relief?' she repeated dully. 'Of course, you would think that . . .'

And so should I, she thought. I should be glad that there is no child to quarrel over. I should be pleased that there will be no tiny person to remind me of what was, of what could have been.

'But I'm not glad about it at all,' she said harshly. 'I'm not pleased——' She left the doctor's office, walking blindly in the heat of the afternoon, not even thinking of where she was going. She should go back to the office, but she couldn't bear the thought of working now. Each separate cell of her body seemed to be tingling under an irregular pattern of electrical shocks that made her want to just start screaming and never stop.

She found herself in the lobby of the apartment block; she nodded curtly to the doorman and almost ran to the lift. I have to get home, she thought, where I can be alone, before I start to cry.

She closed her eyes to hold the tears back. 'I would give everything I have to be carrying his child,' she whispered painfully. A child would bind Rob to her for ever; it would make sure that no matter what he did or where he went, he could never close Shauna completely out of his life again. He wasn't like her father, who had walked away from her, or Greg, who had ignored his son. Rob would never turn his back on any child——

If I had his child, she thought, I could hold him . . .

What kind of a woman am I, she asked herself in horror, to actually consider bringing a baby into the world for a hideous, selfish reason like that? Am I really as self-centred as my mother is, thinking only of my own desires? If I really loved him, I would want him to be happy.

What I want, she admitted painfully, is for him to love me. And that's the one thing I cannot buy, and I cannot demand. It is the one thing I cannot have.

Louise was hoovering in the living-room. She shut the machine off when Shauna came in, and stood in the middle of the room, her hands on her hips. 'Just how long is this game of musical wardrobes going to go on, anyway?' she demanded.

Shauna hardly heard her. She licked her dry lips. 'Why?'

'Doctor Rob is back there packing up his things.' Louise sounded aggravated. 'I've never seen such a pair of newlyweds—— '

'You're not likely to, ever again, either. Be glad of it, Louise.' Shauna didn't look back, but she knew Louise stood there with a puzzled, half-angry look as she walked away.

He's here, she was thinking. But it's only the middle of the afternoon——

She went straight to the little room at the end of the hall. A suitcase lay open on the bed, and Rob was laying piles of shirts into it. He looked up at her—with a shade of guilt in his face, she thought—and went back to his packing. His hands moved smoothly, efficiently. His warm, strong, beautiful hands, she thought, remembering the way he had caressed her...

'I thought you weren't leaving till next week.' It came out in an accusing tone.

'I found a place that's empty, so I can move right away.'

'Were you trying to avoid me?' She braced her hands on the back of his desk chair, mostly to keep herself from trembling. The picture of Amy from their wedding was still there, she noted, tacked neatly to the wall above his desk at eye level.

'No,' he said reasonably. 'It's my regular afternoon off.'

'I suppose you're planning to leave me with the chore of explaining it to Mandy, after you're gone.'

'I'll talk to her as soon as she gets home from school.' He sounded as if he was having trouble keeping his voice level. 'I never have left the difficult parts to you, Shauna—why would I start now?'

'Oh? Does that mean you think I'm doing a lousy job with her?'

He stopped for a few seconds and looked thoughtfully at her. Then he picked up a box and started stacking books in it. 'You're certainly touchy today. What are you doing at home in the middle of the afternoon, anyway?'

She started to shrug the question off. Then she thought, why not let him suffer a little of what I've had to? 'I just saw my doctor.'

She thought for an instant that she saw concern in his eyes but, if it was there, it was quickly shuttered.

'Funny things, pregnancy tests,' she said, very clearly.

He dropped a stack of books. The thud of the heavy volumes on the carpet was satisfying, somehow; it sounded like her heart had felt, when she had got the results of the test.

He stared at her for a long moment.

'It was negative,' she said.

He stooped and began to pick up the books. 'I'm sure that's a comfort to you.'

'Yes.' It sounded sad, but it was the truth, she realised; once her initial disappointment had passed, common sense had come back. A child has a right to two parents, she thought—two people who love him and each other, not just a pair of accidental biological partners.

'You don't have to pretend to be sorry, Shauna.'

She wanted to throw something at him so that he would hurt too. 'Of course I'm not sorry,' she said in a brittle tone. 'If there had been a baby, I would have had to buy you off again——'

'You couldn't have done it.'

'Why not?' she said bitterly. 'I've bought and paid for you once——'

'Don't you think I have any pride at all? Your damned cheque is in this mess somewhere—would you like to have it back as a souvenir?'

'My cheque?' She swung around to face him.

'Yes—your wedding gift to me.' His voice was mocking.

'Do you mean you haven't cashed it? Why on earth not?'

'Because I'd rather pay my debts with the work of my own hands, even if that's the slow way.'

'That money wasn't to pay off your loans,' she said blankly. 'I'd already done that.'

He stopped dead, his hands full of books, and stared at her. 'Then what the hell was it for?'

'I told you! To buy your share in the practice.' Her voice started to tremble. 'Laugh if you want, Rob, but it was a genuine wedding gift——'

'I don't care what it was, I have no intention of taking any of your money. Not one thin dime of it. I'll pay back every cent, Shauna, just as soon as I can, with regular bank interest.'

'But you earned it, Rob!'

He swung around to face her. 'In your bed? I'm glad that my performance satisfied you, Shauna, but I am not a damned gigolo, and I would much rather forget that I ever made love to you!' He sealed the box with packing tape and reached for another empty carton.

'But——'

'Leave it alone, would you, dammit?'

It hurt her to hear the pain in his voice. That's my fault, too, she thought. I do want him to be happy; that, above everything else, is important. And some day maybe I can find some comfort in knowing that I helped to make it possible...

'No, Rob,' she said, 'I won't leave it alone. Please don't talk about paying the money back; we made an agreement——'

'You made the damned agreement. You and that flaky lawyer of yours——'

She raised her voice. 'And as for the cheque, it was a gift. I meant it to buy your partnership, but if you'd rather use it to pay for the rest of your training, that's all right too.'

'Why, Lady Bountiful?' he asked savagely. 'Do you want me to get out of town?'

'No, Rob. I want you to be happy.'

He hurled a book against the wall. A watercolour painting shuddered and swung wildly and settled back against the plaster at an odd angle. 'If the next thing you say is, "Can't we be friends, Rob," I will strangle you.'

Was this the man who had held her so gently that last morning, and then had made her nearly scream with pleasure with his lovemaking? 'I wouldn't suggest it,' she said quietly. 'I think it's obvious that we can't.'

'Well, I only take loans from friends. So keep your blasted money.'

The sarcastic tone tore at her flesh. 'If I want to invest in you instead of in stocks and bonds, why shouldn't I?' she demanded. 'It's going to be awfully expensive, isn't it? Years and years before you're finished with your train-ing——'

'I am not going back to school; I am staying in St Louis. I've already bought a share of the practice.' He looked up from the box. 'In case you're wondering, I found a banker who thinks I'm a good risk.'

'Oh, Rob.' She was honestly upset. 'Perhaps it isn't too late—when did you do it?'

'Four weeks ago today. I was going to tell you, but you didn't seem to care.' He sealed another box and dropped it into the stack on the floor.

Four weeks ago, she thought. That was before Jessica had come back to town, and before he had known that he didn't have to finish the year of their agreement——

'I'm sorry, Rob. They won't let you change your mind?'

'Damn it, Shauna, I don't want to back out. Of course I've thought about specialising, but what I've always wanted is a general practice with all kinds of kids. That's not very ambitious, perhaps, but it's my life. The only thing that held me back was fear of going deeper in debt——' He turned away, and said, more softly, 'But then you said something about having faith in myself, and I knew you were right. So I did it—on my own. I don't need your money, Shauna——'

No, she thought sadly. Not my money, nor anything else.

She glanced up at the photograph above his desk. 'You're not going with Amy, then.'

He followed her gaze, and reached up to pluck the picture from the wall. 'No—and she doesn't understand any more than you do.' He looked down at the glossy paper, cupped in the palm of his brown hand. 'She's absolutely single-minded, and she doesn't understand that not everyone else is. Some day Amy will be the best paediatrician in the world when it comes to premature babies——'

Her heart ached for him—it was so obvious that looking at the photograph hurt him. 'That doesn't mean she won't ever change,' she said. Her voice shook a little. 'She does love you, Rob, and some day——' And I hope I never have to know it, her heart cried.

He gritted his teeth. 'Damn you, Shauna McCoy,' he said. 'You've shredded my pride a thousand different ways, but that is the worst.'

The accusation startled her. 'I don't understand.'

'You never have.' Deliberately, he ripped the photograph in half, and then tore it over and over until it was a mass of unrecognisable fragments in a heap on the desk blotter. 'I was a damned fool, Shauna. I saw what I wanted to see.'

She nodded, but she didn't understand. She slipped the engagement ring off her finger and laid it next to the ruined photograph on the blotter. The canary-yellow diamond winked up at her.

He turned then, and saw it. 'What's that all about?'

'You wouldn't take my wedding gift. I don't want yours.' She stared at the blotter. 'Rob—why did you tear the picture up?'

'What difference does it make?'

'One hell of a lot, to me!' Her hands were clenched hard; questions had started to circle madly in her brain. 'Why won't you take the money?'

'Would you have the decency to get out of here now, and let me finish my packing?'

'Not till I get answers, Rob. If it wasn't the money, then why did you marry me?'

'Do you mean you've never wondered before?'

She shook her head. 'Of course not. I kept the agreement. I thought you knew I had.' She looked up at him, and whispered, 'Why, Rob?'

'Why did you insist on putting the money into the agreement?' he countered. 'I told you I didn't want it.'

'Because I didn't think I had anything else to offer you,' she admitted, very softly.

There was a long silence. Her eyes prickled with tears. 'And I was right, wasn't I?' she said. There was no accusation left in her, only hurt, and a desperate need to understand. 'You can't wait to get away from me. But

I still don't understand why you won't take the money. Rob, please tell me——'

He released a long, defeated sigh. 'You made your bargain,' he said quietly, 'and I agreed to your terms, because I knew if I didn't, you'd go find someone else to marry you. I was damned if I was going to let that happen.'

'But——' She sat down abruptly in the chair beside his desk. It almost tipped over, but she didn't notice. She swallowed hard, and croaked, 'You *wanted* to marry me?'

'Oh, yes. Humorous, isn't it?'

'No,' she whispered. It can't be true, she thought. It's a lovely lie——

'I've always imagined the woman I'd marry some day,' he mused, 'but I've never had time to try to find her—and I never had much to offer her, either. But I didn't dream that one day I would walk into an examining-room to see a little girl with a stomach-ache, and find that all I could think of was her sister's eyes, and how much I wanted to take the pins out of her hair and let it fall into a veil for only me to see——'

'My God,' she said. 'You didn't seem to know I was there——'

'I fought it, Shauna. I told myself I was crazy; Mandy said you were engaged. But I ended up in your office a few days later because I couldn't stay away from you any longer, and then I could have kicked myself for falling in love with someone who didn't need anything, especially not a disorganised slob of a paediatrician——'

Hope was fluttering deep within her, as fragile as a butterfly's wing.

'And then you made your crazy proposition, and I gambled. And I lost. I lost my heart. And my soul, and very nearly my mind——'

That day in the Japanese gardens, she remembered, he had said that he was taking a chance, that he had a lot to lose—— I have been so terribly blind, she thought.

'Dammit, Shauna, there were so many things that let me believe you weren't as cold-blooded about it as you seemed. There was Mandy, and the way you nearly cried over the orchids on our wedding day. Then there was the night when you rubbed my back, and gave yourself so completely to me that I thought surely it was only a matter of time——' He slammed a fist down on his desk. 'When I found out you'd only done it because you felt sorry for me, you can't imagine how that hurt!'

'It wasn't that at all.'

He stopped dead. 'It wasn't?'

'No.' She stood up, carefully, half expecting that her knees would be too wobbly to hold her. 'I think I fell in love with you in a Japanese garden, Rob. But I didn't even know it, then. And when I realised what had happened to me, I was afraid that when it was all over, and you walked away——'

'As if I could, dammit!' His hands came to rest on her shoulders. 'Every day I told myself I ought to just walk out of your life—but I couldn't. And every night I came back to you, because I couldn't stay away. I want you so badly that it tears me up to be in the same room with you——'

She laughed, tremulously. 'Would you stop shaking me, Rob? My teeth are coming loose——'

'I'm sorry——' Then he swore softly and pulled her close against him, so abruptly that the breath was knocked from her, but it didn't matter because there was no need to breathe any more, and in any case there was no oxygen left in the world so there was no point in trying to breathe——

And when, finally, she could think again, she whispered, 'Amy told me I was a fool, that night we quarrelled, and I called her apartment to see if you were there. How very right she was.'

'She did?' He seemed startled. 'She told me the same thing, you know. That was the morning I signed the papers to buy into the practice——'

Shauna thought about it. 'The day after we first made love?' she questioned softly. 'Was that why——'

'Why I felt confident enough to take a step like that?' He nodded. 'I broke it to Amy at lunch that day. I was so happy—you and I had been so close the night before, and the first chance you gave me I was going to drag you off to a quiet place and negotiate a new agreement— a real marriage instead of the kind your mother had taught you about.'

'And I met you with silence, and suspicion, and doubt,' she whispered.

'Yeah,' he said. 'If you'd hit me with an axe I couldn't have been more stunned, Shauna.'

'I was afraid——' She had trusted him at first, she realised, when it didn't matter. But then the stakes had grown too high, and she had had too much to lose, and so she had thrown everything away because she could not bear to take a chance—not even on Rob, who must surely be the most trustworthy man she would ever know...

She couldn't put it into words. She held him tightly to her, wanting never to let him go.

'If you'll excuse me——' It was cool, polite. From the corner of her eye, Shauna could see a dark-haired, be-spectacled child standing in the doorway. She uttered a soft moan and moved the barest fraction of an inch away from Rob. She was firmly pulled back against his chest.

'Surely you don't think that I will ever let you go again?' he whispered.

She smiled. 'Please don't.'

He looked down into her eyes, and caught his breath. 'Go away, Mandy,' he said unsteadily.

'It looks as if you're the one who's planning to do that.' Mandy's face was tight, as if she couldn't quite decide whether to be angry or frightened. 'Louise wants to know how many will be here for dinner.'

'Three,' Rob said, firmly.

'From now on, there will always be three,' Shauna said.

'I wouldn't bet on that,' Rob murmured. 'There might be four, or five——' He kissed her hard. 'I have to admit that in the moment before you told me the results of your test, I was thinking fondly of a little girl with your long, red hair and my orderly habits——'

'Poor child,' Shauna murmured.

'Not at all. She'll have experienced parents, and a wonderful big sister——'

Shauna turned her head to look at Mandy. 'I thought you were reporting to Louise,' she reminded her.

'What are all the boxes for?' Mandy demanded.

Rob looked at the piles of cartons and sighed. 'To pack away all our foolishness,' he said.

'That doesn't make any sense at all,' Mandy complained.

Rob pulled her into their embrace. 'I'll explain it later.'

Louise appeared in the doorway. 'How many chops shall I——' She stopped. 'Does this mean I have to move all those clothes again?' she wailed.

'For the last time, Louise,' Shauna promised.

The housekeeper groaned. 'Come on, Mandy,' she ordered. 'It's obvious they don't need any company just now.'

Rob grinned. 'Shall we take all this stuff out of the boxes before you change your mind again?'

'I never will.' Shauna picked up her diamond ring and slipped it contentedly back on to her finger. 'I'll get you another copy of that photo,' she said. 'I don't mind, now, if you have Amy's picture on your wall.'

'I didn't put it up there because of Amy.' She raised an eyebrow, and he said, 'It was because you looked so flaming jealous that it gave me hope——'

She was smiling when he kissed her.

'I loved you first,' he whispered.

'I love you more.'

'Would you like to prove that?'

Shauna put her head down on his shoulder. 'I can try. But it might take a while—like the rest of your life.'

'That's all right,' Rob said. 'I'm not going anywhere.'

ANNOUNCING . . .

The Lost Moon Flower
by Bethany Campbell

Look for it this August
wherever Harlequins are sold

HR 3000-1

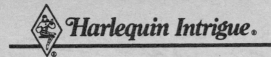

They went in through the terrace door. The house was dark, most of the servants were down at the circus, and only Nelbert's hired security guards were in sight. It was child's play for Blackheart to move past them, the work of two seconds to go through the solid lock on the terrace door. And then they were creeping through the darkened house, up the long curving stairs, Ferris fully as noiseless as the more experienced Blackheart.

They stopped on the second floor landing. "What if they have guns?" Ferris mouthed silently.

Blackheart shrugged. "Then duck."

"How reassuring," she responded. Footsteps directly above them signaled that the thieves were on the move, and so should they be.

For more romance, suspense and adventure, read Harlequin Intrigue. Two exciting titles each month, available wherever Harlequin Books are sold.

INTA-1

Harlequin Regency Romance™

Romance the way it was *always* meant to be!

The time is 1811, when a Regent Prince rules the empire. The place is London, the glittering capital where rakish dukes and dazzling debutantes scheme and flirt in a dangerously exciting game. Where marriage is the passport to wealth and power, yet every girl hopes secretly for love....

Welcome to Harlequin Regency Romance where reading is an adventure and romance is *not* just a thing of the past! Two delightful books a month.

Available wherever Harlequin Books are sold.